The Power of Love

The Power of Love
(or… If wishes could only come true)

Phyllis J. Burton

Bridge House

British Library Cataloguing in Publication Data
A Record of this Publication is available from the British
Library

ISBN 978-1-907335-72-3

This edition published 2019 by Bridge House Publishing
Manchester, England

Acknowledgement
A big thank you to Gill James, Editor of Bridge House
Publishing, for her valuable help and encouragement.

I dedicate this book to my husband Jim, and all the members of my family, for their love and patience during the writing of these love stories.

My beauty is as boundless as the sea,
My love as deep, the more I give to thee,
The more I have, for both are infinite.

(Romeo and Juliet – Shakespeare 1564 -1616)

CONTENTS

ALL FOR THE LOVE OF ANNA

As soon as Henry Bawdson woke up, he knew he was totally hooked. He was hopelessly in love with Anna.

Last night, Henry had celebrated his fortieth birthday with Anna, and several of his closest friends. It was now 7.30 a.m. and a slight, but persistent headache, as a result of drinking too much, was trying its hardest to mar what had been a really good evening, but it wasn't succeeding. He'd really enjoyed himself, especially after their friends had gone home, and he was at last left alone with Anna. Henry's heartbeat quickened when he remembered their first almost clumsy attempts at love-making, and he smiled. Anna was wonderful, and there had to be some compensation for being so old.

Anna had left his flat in the early hours of the morning, and for some time afterwards Henry had been unable to sleep. Thoughts about what he had to do in a few hours' time, and his ever-present thoughts about Anna, wouldn't go away. Visions of her face swam before him like an irresistible treat set before a starving man, and they'd twisted and wormed their way into his subconscious mind.

Henry squinted at the digital clock beside his bed. The green flashing numbers reminded him of today's task. It was an important day and high time he was up. He yawned, stretched his arms above his head, and climbed out of the warmth of his bed.

He couldn't even face eating breakfast, but instead he made himself a cup of strong, black filter coffee, before returning to his bedroom, and flopping down on his bed to drink it. The delicious aroma spread itself around the bedroom, and he sipped it slowly, all the while thinking about the night before. He couldn't believe that Anna wanted to be with him as much as he wanted, and needed,

10

to be with her. It must be love, he told himself, because everyone knows that not being able to sleep and not wanting to eat are just two of the symptoms.

He sighed deeply, yawned, and then shook his head. It was some time since he'd allowed a girl to get under his skin like this. Not since... Kate...

Henry's mood plummeted downwards.

Henry had adored his partner, Kate. He believed that she understood his passion for music, and his need to perform. But in reality, she didn't! She left him after his most triumphant concert performance ever, and as a result, he vowed never to play the piano again. Kate's decision to leave him had come so quickly, that Henry hardly had any time to take a breath.

He remembered the concert, and its aftermath, so well...

It was held in a grand hall in the centre of London, and Henry had just completed his final solo performance of Grieg's Piano Concerto in A minor. The beautiful grand piano overlooked hundreds of ecstatic cheering people, and they were all calling out his name. "Henry Bawdson", "Bravo" and "Encore... Encore!" People were standing up and applauding noisily whilst stamping their feet, and others were waving their programmes in the air. Henry felt intoxicated by the warmth from the audience, and his heart swelled with pride.

He'd been at the pinnacle of his success; everyone wanted to be part of his life as a concert pianist. Even his agent used to laughingly complain about the amount of work he had to do in order to keep up with Henry's growing popularity. Interviews on television almost became the norm, and his photograph was all over the Internet. But in the end, because of Kate, it didn't bring him any happiness.

11

Thinking about all that past fame and glory always upset Henry. He recalled what happened in his dressing room directly after his successful concert was over. His heart had been filled with emotion and happiness as he'd left the auditorium. He felt proud of his performance, and was looking forward to celebrating with Kate, but this was not meant to be. Instead, she entered the room with her lips set in a cold, determined line, and it had sent shivers down his spine. She didn't even congratulate him, or say that she'd enjoyed the concert. She simply stood there, before saying the words that turned his success into a total nightmare…

'Henry, there is only one way I can say this to you, but I…'

'What's the matter, Kate?' Henry's heart began to leap in his chest. 'Has something dreadful happened?'

'No, nothing has happened at all, and that's the problem.' Kate continued, holding her hands out with her palms uppermost.

Henry was sitting in front of a large mirror with bright lights all around the edge. Over the years, he'd sat in many dressing rooms in front of mirrors like this one. He looked at his reflection, but all he could see was Kate standing behind him. Her usually pretty face was a cold unfriendly mask, with no feeling or emotion at all. Henry's heart missed a beat, and he turned round to face her.

'Please tell me what's wrong then, Kate? I don't understand. This isn't like you at all.'

'Henry you must have noticed a change in our relationship recently.' She turned her head away. 'It isn't going anywhere, is it? When do we ever go out and have fun?'

'Fun? But I thought you loved my music, Kate.' Henry looked away. He felt hurt, crestfallen, and surprised. He

12

couldn't imagine that she could ever say such hurtful things
to him. He turned round to face her, and sighed deeply.
'You are right of course, but I've ... I've been so busy
rehearsing, and preparing for concerts and interviews.'

Kate looked at him in despair. 'And don't I just know it,
and that of course is the problem.' Henry started to say
something, but she interrupted him. 'You haven't any time
left for me. The only important thing in your life, is your
music!'

'But... I thought you understood what my life involved.'
Henry felt desperate, as he realised what she was about to
say.

'I'm sorry Henry, I can't take any more of this, and
that's why I'm moving out of the flat tomorrow. I must
apologise for being so blunt, but I'm moving up to
Manchester. My new job starts next week.'

Henry felt numb, and desolate after Kate had gone. His life
lost all its meaning, and he knew his piano playing
extravaganza was at an end. He couldn't see a time when
he would want, or need, to play the piano again; in fact he
didn't even want to look at one anymore. 'Pianos – urgh…
I never want to go near one again,' he remembered saying
to some friends.

Even though the memory of Kate's cold words brought
back the pain Henry felt at the time, he knew it was
destructive. He tried to force the fact that he didn't ever
wish to play the piano again to the back of his mind, but it
refused to go away. Just thinking about how his fingers
used to run expertly over the keyboard caused beads of
perspiration to form on his forehead, and Henry could feel
it running down his face. Everyone had told him that he
created memorable and beautiful music.

Henry hadn't played the piano for such a long time, and

he shuddered when he looked down at his fingers. They were trembling, and reminded him of plump sausages. He closed his eyes.

And then along came Anna.

Her face swam before him. She always had the ability to make him feel better, and often tried to encourage him to play the piano again. He shook his head. Could he run his fingers over a keyboard, and create beautiful music again? Perhaps he would find out later that day, he thought, as he picked up his cup from the bedside table.

His mobile phone trilled suddenly, making him jump, and causing him to spill coffee down his new white towelling robe. It had been a present from Anna. He cursed under his breath and reached for the phone. Who would be calling him so early, he wondered? Then he smiled. It was probably Anna. His heart began to beat faster.

'Hello, lover boy,' she said. 'How are you this morning?' The sound of her languorous voice sent Henry's senses reeling; it sounded like warm velvet.

'Hi,' he replied. 'I'm fine, but... I miss you.'

'I miss you too, Henry darling. Don't forget to pick me up at 7.30 this evening will you? I know you have a lot on your mind today, and I'm sending you a really big hug.'

'Thank you Anna. Yes, I do have a lot on my mind, but it's mostly about you.'

'I wish,' Anna replied with a laugh.

'It's true. Anyway, I must get on,' Henry said feeling reluctant even to tear himself away from her voice. 'I'll see you this evening then. Oh, yes and wear that pink outfit you wore last night, it really suits you; in fact it makes you look...' Henry took a deep breath as his mind began to wander... 'Bye my darling.'

'Bye, Henry, and... good luck today.'

'Thanks,' Henry replied dryly. 'I need more than luck, Anna. I need a miracle.'

Later, Henry stood outside the double wooden doors that lead into the George Hetherington Memorial Hall. Even though it was pouring with rain, he was reluctant to enter the building because he knew what was waiting for him.

'Go inside Henry. Please go inside, you know you can do it,' Anna's voice seemed to insist inside his head.

The people who lived in the village of Alvington were immensely proud of their Memorial Hall. It stood elegantly on the edge of the village green, and reminded everyone that it was built to commemorate all the people who had perished during the two World Wars. But to Henry it was a huge mental obstacle. If he could just conquer his fear of failure by taking this first step on the way to recovery, then he knew deep down the rest would come easily. He tried to take his mind off what he was about to do, and thought about being with Anna last night instead. He really loved her, and he was doing this for her.

A stream of water from a gutter way above his head, chose that moment to pour down on top of him, reminding him of his task. He mopped his head with his handkerchief, and tried to keep his mind on what he had to do. Only this wooden door now stood between him and his destiny. He twisted the doorknob, and pushed it slightly. The hinges let out a creak reminiscent of the cry of a banshee, which only deepened his inner turmoil.

Henry entered the hall, walked a few steps, and looked around him. He was greeted by an eerie silence, and once again fear grabbed hold of him. He could hear his heart beating in his ears, and his legs began to shake. His eyes fastened upon an impressive grand piano. His heart now began to pound even faster, making him feel slightly dizzy, and his breath seemed to catch in his throat. 'I can't do this,' he said as he turned round, and began to walk back the way he'd come.

Anna's image once more swam before his eyes. She seemed to be urging him on. How could he resist her pleas. He would do anything for her, he decided.

Henry's heart now raced for a different reason, as he thought about her. He considered her to be beautiful, but some of his friends didn't agree with him, of course. But what did they know? She wore glasses, yes, but then he did as well. Her nose was less than straight, but then curiously enough, his own nose was a bit crooked, and it had never bothered him. What Anna might have lacked in the looks department, she certainly made up for in other ways. She was aware of her own sensuality and great fun to be with. She was kind, and nothing was too much trouble for her.

But above all, Henry knew that, unlike Kate, Anna understood him. She shared his love of music, and what's more she understood his frustration over his inability, or reluctance, to play the piano. In fact, she seemed to know him even better than he knew himself. Henry decided that he was going to ask Anna to marry him, tonight. He loved her so much, and he was convinced that she would accept his proposal. He looked around the cavernous room, but first, he had to prove that he could make beautiful music again.

The large, black grand piano sat in a corner of the hall like a predatory spider, and he approached it with mounting apprehension. As a child, Henry's one joy had been to place his fingers on a keyboard to create sounds, tunes, melodies and fragments of music he'd heard. These sounds would flow through his mind like a river, and come out through his fingers, thus sweeping away all his childish cares and fears.

He could almost hear the sound of his teacher's voice.
'Henry, Henry, my child… that was beautiful,' Miss Humberston would say in her high, piping soprano tone. *'You could charm the birds off the trees with your playing. Now don't forget to practice every day, will you? If you do, I am quite certain that you will be performing in all the major concert halls throughout the world.'*

She would sit down beside him, with her hands neatly folded in her lap, her eyes closed in ecstasy. Miss Humberston had been right of course.

Henry remembered the crowded halls, the noise, the smells, the excitement and above all, the music. It had tantalised and intoxicated him then. If only… if only, he thought. He sat down on the stool, and then stood up again to adjust the height. His long thin legs always seemed to present a problem. He looked down at the keyboard, and its challenging teeth appeared to grin at him. *'Play me, if you can,'* they seemed to say. Why did he always feel this way? What was wrong with him? Was even this piano testing his resolve? Henry could feel his glasses beginning to slip down his nose, and he pushed them up again. He took a deep breath… and thought about Anna. Her face swam before his eyes yet again, cutting out all external influences.

'Yes, I can do it,' Henry told himself, and he placed his fingers on the keys…

At first, the sound they produced jarred on Henry's nerves, and his teeth clamped together like two pieces of fused metal. He groaned as the discordant vibrations travelled throughout his body, but he knew that he had to tame this wooden monster with its stark and unfriendly teeth. After a while, and to his amazement, he began to enjoy himself. He thrilled at the long forgotten feeling of immense power he used to derive from just running his

17

fingers over the keys, until he finally ended with a dramatic flourish with his arms raised.

Henry's music inspired mind felt refreshed and confident. He knew he'd fought this piano and had won! A feeling of exhilaration almost like an electric current, passed through him. He stood up, and punched the air in triumph.

'Yeeees,' he shouted. 'I knew I could do it.'

An elderly woman pushed her way through a tatty floor-length curtain just below the small stage, and entered the hall. She looked at him with a worried expression on her face.

'Mr. Bawdson?' she enquired. 'Is everything alright?'

'Yes, everything is just fine,' Henry said beaming at her.

'Good. I'm pleased to meet you at last. I'm Ethel Jones, the caretaker. I'm sorry I wasn't here when you arrived. The bus was late.' She walked over to the piano and looked down at the keys. 'I can't thank you enough Mr. Bawdson. The last time it was used it sounded dreadful, and the committee members were starting to think that we needed to buy a new one.'

'Well, there's no need to worry anymore, Mrs. Jones,' he said beaming at her from ear to ear. 'A few of the keys were sticking that's all, and I've tuned it to concert pitch as you requested.'

'Thank you.'

It was a real pleasure, Mrs. Jones, believe me. It's a beautiful piano,' he said. 'Well, I must be on my way, goodbye.' He stood up, smiled at her, and strode confidently towards the door feeling really exhilarated. He could almost hear the sound of the words *"Encore... encore... encore"*. He was back!

'Thank you, Anna!'

BRUSH WITH LOVE

'Conchita, my little sister, I must talk to you.' Conchita Gonzalez was preparing the evening meal for herself and her two brothers. Her elder brother, Carlos, sat by the fire looking at her with a worried expression on his swarthy, but handsome, face.

'Conchita, this is important, so will you please listen to what I have to say?'

'Yes Carlos?' she answered, her large eyes opening wide and filled with innocence. 'Is there a problem?' She continued to stir the contents of a huge, black pot which was suspended over a blazing fire. A delicious aroma spread enticingly around the room making her feel hungry. She wondered what Carlos could possibly have to say to her, because as far as she was aware, she hadn't done anything to incur his anger, or his disapproval.

The room was hot and airless. Carlos didn't answer immediately, but rose from his chair and walked over to a rough wooden stand underneath the window. Was he keeping her in suspense on purpose, Conchita wondered? She watched him as he took off his shirt before picking up a large, but cracked, white jug containing cold water, and poured it into a bowl. After washing himself noisily he grabbed hold of a nearby cloth, and having completed his ablutions, he glared at her before sitting down in his chair again.

'I've heard some disturbing rumours,' he said whilst folding the cloth and hanging it on the back of his chair. He looked at her with complete distain.

'Rumours,' Conchita replied, her eyes suddenly becoming wary. 'What kind of rumours?'

'I've heard from some of my male friends that Senor Fernandez is now using nude models,' he replied. 'Is this

19

true?' Conchita took a deep breath as he continued. 'Also that his morals, and his lifestyle aren't all they should be. As the eldest member of this family since our father's death, I feel it's my duty to see that you don't come to any harm.'

'Harm, Carlos, but I don't understand. You surely don't think that I would...'

'Please don't interrupt. I understand that you've been sitting for him.'

'Yes, I have, but I still don't see what you are so worried about.'

'This is important Conchita, so please listen to me. I hope you haven't been posing in the nude, because if you have, I'm afraid it will be the last time you go anywhere near him.'

'No Carlos. I've always been dressed in our traditional Spanish costume,' she answered indignantly, holding her head up high. 'I'm positive that he wouldn't ask me to do such a thing.'

'Is Senor Fernandez not a real man then, this... this paintbrush wielding artist of yours? Isn't he a man with full-blooded feelings?' There was an ugly sneer on his handsome face. He shifted his large, well-built frame in his chair, and began to stare into the dancing flames of the fire beneath the cooking pot.

Conchita's younger brother, Pablo, was sitting in his usual chair reading, and he looked confused as he looked up at his brother. 'Rumours, Carlos? Should you believe in mere rumours? I don't think so. I have met Francisco Fernandez once or twice recently, and he seems cultured and genuine,' he said. 'I believe Conchita when she says she's been sitting for him in traditional Spanish costume. Why are you insulting her in this way?'

Conchita looked lovingly at her brother. 'Thank you, Pablo.'

20

Carlos glared at both of them. 'My friends have told me some worrying things about him, and I don't take these rumours, or whatever you would like to call them, lightly.' Pablo wasn't spoiling for a fight with his brother and shrugged his shoulders, before turning back to his book.

Conchita was a beautiful young woman with long black hair that hung gently around her shoulders. She wore a long flowing dress, the bodice of which was low cut, and her bosom heaved with hurt and emotion. Her skin glistened with perspiration, and her large brown eyes flashed with anger at her brother's insinuations. She tossed her hair over her shoulder and placed her hands on her hips. 'Carlos, how dare you insult Francisco? He's a gentleman. He is...'

'What Conchita? What is he... your lover perhaps?'

She felt insulted. 'My lover! I can't believe that you could even think that I could do such a thing.'

Carlos stood up. He was tall and towered over her as he grabbed hold of her wrist. 'As I said, there have been certain rumours.'

'Please let go. You're hurting me.'

'Our father would have been most displeased if he'd known you were consorting with such a man. I forbid...'

'I refuse to listen to you,' Conchita said, struggling to get away from him. 'Our father is now dead, if you remember? I'm going to my room.' She turned and ran through the door. She could hear her brothers arguing as she raced up the old wooden stairs, and she spent the rest of the evening alone, leaving her two brothers to fend for themselves.

Conchita went to bed early, but because she still felt so confused, she couldn't sleep.

'How dare Carlos forbid me to see Francisco?' she cried out. Her mind was filled with righteous indignation as she peered into the gathering gloom. But supposing he's right?

She could never sit for any man without any clothes on. She knew that she couldn't even think of doing such a thing. She decided to speak to Francisco about it when she saw him the next day.

The following morning Conchita left the house early before her brothers were awake. Her anger towards Carlos still hadn't diminished. 'Surely,' she asked herself, 'in this year of 1801, I should be able to make some of the decisions affecting my own life?' The narrow streets of Madrid were stiflingly hot and sultry, as the buildings released the heat they'd absorbed from days of high temperatures. She walked around for a long time, before finally making her way to the Artists' House which Francisco Fernandez shared with some of his friends.

Over the last couple of months, Conchita had been slowly falling in love with Francisco. The portrait he was painting of her was nearing completion, and she was trying to place this thought to the back of her mind. 'Francisco is the kindest, most passionate and romantic person I've ever met,' she said to herself. 'Carlos has no right to criticise him.' As Conchita walked along the hot narrow streets leading to the Artists' House, she became even more angry with her brother. Francisco's studio was crammed with portraits both finished and unfinished, but as far as she was aware there were no nude paintings among them. In addition, his bookshelves contained volumes about the life and work of many writers throughout the ages. He was a sensitive and intelligent man, so how dare Carlos say such things about him, she thought as she walked along the narrow streets. But a little worm of doubt still presented itself in her brain.

Conchita felt hot and flustered. Even though the sun was still quite low in the sky, she couldn't wait to get inside the quiet coolness of the studio. She stopped outside the old rambling building, took a deep breath, and walked into the courtyard. A cool fountain splashed and gurgled merrily in the centre, reminding Conchita of an oasis in a desert. The whole area was dotted with potted palms, and other Mediterranean plants.

She heard a voice above her head, and she looked upwards. Francisco was watering a window box, and some of the water was dripping slowly downwards.

'Conchita, my little bird,' he called out. 'You're early this morning, but never mind do come up.' Her heart fluttered wildly as she walked up the narrow staircase. She knocked on the old wooden door, and Francisco opened it with an artistic flourish. She thought he looked deliciously handsome in his artist's smock, and the floppy cap which he always wore was placed at a jaunty angle. His teeth glowed white as his brown skin creased into a welcoming smile. 'My beautiful Conchita,' he said giving her a little bow, 'please do come in?'

'Thank you, Francisco.'

'Your clothes are over there as usual,' he said, looking at her keenly before kissing her on both cheeks. 'You are looking tired. Are those two brothers of yours working you too hard?'

'No, no of course not, I... I didn't sleep well last night that's all.' She pulled her hair back, and secured it with a large black comb to support the black lace headdress.

'Conchita you're not a slave and you mustn't let them walk all over you. It's not right.' He walked over to his easel, and started sorting through his paints and brushes. 'Before we start, I would like to talk to you. Now that I've nearly finished this portrait, I was wondering if you would consider sitting for me again. We could try something different this time.'

Her brother's harsh words came back to Conchita, and her heart thumped wildly.

'I asked if you'd mind trying something new,' he said as he walked back to her side. 'Why are you so inattentive this morning?'

'I'm sorry.' She turned away, as hot prickly tears began to fall down her cheeks.

'My dear Conchita, what's wrong? What have I said, or even done?' he demanded gently.

'I can't sit for you without any clothes on. I could never do such a thing,' she said between sobs.

Francisco looked confused. 'You, sitting for me without any clothes on, Conchita? I don't under…'

Conchita interrupted him. 'My brother Carlos said that you were only interested in painting nude portraits now. He's forbidden me to come here, if that's what you want me to do.'

'I could never do that to you, my sweet one.' He walked towards her with his arms open wide. 'Yes, I do want to paint another portrait of you, but in a different pose and costume. I want to catch some of the raw passion I can see in your eyes.' He drew her into his arms. 'Now, I don't want any more tears, or I'll be unable to finish the portrait.' He sighed. 'But yes, I have to be honest with you; your brother Carlos is right in what he said. My thoughts have been turning towards the nude form for some time. In fact, I already have someone who has agreed to sit for me. She is due to come here later for a second sitting.'

'You have someone else?' Conchita's mouth trembled, and she felt helpless under the intensity of his gaze.

'Yes.' His eyes softened as he looked down at her. 'I could hardly ask the woman I love more than anything in the world, to do something like that.' He knelt down on one knee. 'I've loved you since the first day we met. My

24

dearest, sweetest Conchita, you would do me the greatest honour if you would consent to become my wife?' She could hardly believe her ears. All her wildest dreams had now come true, and her heart hammered inside her chest.

'Well, what do you say, my darling one?'

'Yes, of course I'll marry you Francisco, but... but there's a big problem.' She looked up at him her eyes glistening with tears.

'What's the matter? You love me, don't you?'

Conchita's dark brown eyes suddenly filled with passion. 'Yes of course I love you, Francisco. Isn't it obvious? But Carlos, he...' She was silent for a moment. 'Because of all this gossip, he... he'll never give me his permission to marry you.'

Francisco stood up, and pulled himself up to his full height. 'Do you think that he'll refuse me permission? Me, Francisco Fernandez! I come from a good, wealthy family. I don't think so.' He looked down at her, and his body relaxed. 'I'm sorry, Conchita, but I...'

She interrupted him. 'Carlos promised my father that he would look after me, and he takes this task seriously. Now that he's heard these rumours, I...'

'Don't worry. I'll try to see him tonight.' Francis looked thoughtful for a moment. 'My little Conchita, I will marry you and we will be the happiest two people in the whole wide world.' She flung her arms around his neck and kissed him. He returned her kiss passionately, and soon all thoughts of the portrait were forgotten.

Later, Conchita said goodbye to her beloved Francisco, and as she walked by the fountain in the courtyard, a rather beautiful young woman came in from the narrow street. To Conchita's consternation, she made her way to the wooden steps leading up to Francisco's studio. Her face seemed

25

familiar. She was tall, pretty and had a voluptuous figure. Conchita's forehead creased with worry, as she tried to recall where she'd seen her before. Then she remembered, and her blood ran cold.

'Oh my god… it's Mercedes!'

Mercedes had been walking out with her brother Carlos for a few weeks, and even though they hadn't met, Conchita recognised her. With a rapidly beating heart and burning with curiosity, she stood behind the fountain. The girl climbed the steps leading up to Francisco's apartment, and knocked on the door. Conchita's mind was plunged into turmoil, and she felt sick. Could it be that it was Mercedes who was posing in the nude for him? Conchita knew she couldn't possibly blame Francisco, because he had no idea that she was walking out with Carlos. Nevertheless, it still hurt her to think that his eyes would be looking at the nude form of another woman, especially one as attractive as Mercedes. She tried to push these thoughts away. But others soon came crowding into her mind, and they could not so easily be brushed away.

What would Carlos do if he found out what Mercedes was doing? Bearing in mind his strong disapproval of his sister posing without any clothes on, she couldn't imagine him accepting the same behaviour from Mercedes. 'How can I tell my brother something like that?' she cried. Conchita walked home feeling deeply troubled.

That evening, she sat alone in her room and again retired to bed early. She was torn between her love for Francisco and her duty to Carlos. She heard a cock crowing in the distance just before falling into an exhausted sleep.

The following morning, her brothers were washing themselves in the kitchen when she came downstairs.

'Good morning, Carlos. Good morning Pablo,' she said, averting her gaze.

26

'Good morning, Conchita. Did you sleep well? It was a very hot night,' Pablo said smiling at her.

'Yes, it was.'

'Will you make a start on our breakfasts, please?' Carlos demanded. 'I have a particularly busy day ahead of me.' He was silent for a while, and she watched him as she prepared their breakfast, but she knew from the look on his face that he had something on his mind. 'I met Francisco Fernandez last night. He wishes to marry you, I understand. From what I've heard, he is totally unsuitable for you,' he said with a distinct sneer on his face.

'Yes, Carlos. He proposed to me yesterday,' Conchita answered, quietly holding her breath.

'I have to tell you, that I'm withholding my permission, Conchita.' He looked away.

Anger rose within her. 'But why Carlos? You have no right to do such a thing. **We love one another, and what's more, I'm old enough to make up my own mind,**' she shouted with her hands firmly placed on her hips.

'No right, you say? I have every right. As head of this family, I will not agree to such a union.'

'You are being cruel and unreasonable,' she replied, as she placed some crusty bread on the table.

'I've said my final word on the subject, Conchita. You will not see this man again, and I forbid you ever to go near his house in the future.'

Conchita fled from the room with his words echoing in her ears. She raced upstairs to the sanctuary of her bedroom, slammed the door and burst into tears. 'What can I do?' she sobbed. 'This is all becoming impossible.' Conchita felt totally confused, but she was quite certain that she couldn't tell Carlos about Mercedes. If she did, then he would have even more reason to hate Francisco, and any hope of them being together would be gone forever.

27

Conchita was in a difficult position, because deep down she loved both her brothers, and it saddened her to think that one of them was being deceived. But she loved Francisco. Her heart belonged to him and him alone. She knew that her only way forward was to seek his advice.

Conchita left the house quietly, making sure that Carlos didn't hear or see her, and set off once more to the Artists' House. She raced up the stairs and knocked on the door. Francisco looked tired and concerned as he opened it. She looked at him, and immediately burst into tears. 'Oh Francisco, my brother Carlos is so angry, and he...'

'Conchita, my love, do come inside.' He took a handkerchief from the pocket in his artist's smock and tried to dry her eyes. 'I think I know what the problem is my sweet one, and I hate to see you like this.'

'Carlos told me that he wouldn't give us permission to marry, and... and he's forbidden me ever to see you again.'

'My dear sweet girl, I know all about this too. Carlos was angry with me last night, and I was preparing to come round to see you later, so that we could talk.'

'But Francisco, Carlos wouldn't wish to see you in our house,' she said, as tears streamed down her face once more.

Francisco pulled himself up to his full height. 'I'm not afraid of your brother.' He took her into his arms and kissed her. 'Conchita, I love you and I want to marry you. In fact, I'm going to marry you.'

She was silent for a moment. 'There's a much bigger problem, Francisco.'

'There is?' His brown eyes opened wide in surprise.

'Yes. It's about the girl who came to see you yesterday. Is she the one who is posing in the nude for you?'

'Yes. Her name is Mercedes, but what has this to do with...?'

'Carlos and Mercedes are walking out together, Francisco!'

He pulled away from her, a look of shock passing over his face. 'Ohhh,' he said, closing his eyes in dismay. 'Yes... I see what you mean.' He sighed. 'That's a big problem. I had no idea that she even knew your brother.' He began to pace around the room. After a few minutes, he stopped. 'Well in that case, we have to think of some way to make him change his mind. But what?' He sat down on an old wooden chair with his head in his hands for a while. A few minutes later, he looked up at Conchita with tears in his eyes. 'Perhaps we could... no, he's an intelligent man and I'm sure he would never believe you.'

'What do you mean, Francisco? Carlos only said that he'd heard rumours. He has no proof. Oh what shall we do? I am so scared. He has a nasty temper sometimes, and you could be in danger if he finds out that Mercedes is sitting for you.'

'Mercedes is due to come here for another sitting this morning. We'll have to discuss this with her.'

They sat down together and tried to work out a plan.

Later when Mercedes arrived at the studio, she seemed surprised to see Conchita standing there. Was there a hint of recognition in her gaze, Conchita wondered?

'Mercedes,' Francisco said beckoning her to the nearest chair. 'We have something important to discuss with you, so please come and sit down.'

'Yes, Senor Fernandez.'

'I'd like to introduce you to Conchita. She is Carlos Gonzales' sister, and the woman I intend to marry,' he declared proudly, but his eyes betrayed his concern.

'Carlos's sister. I can't...' The girl looked warily at Conchita, and her face turned pale. She turned to Francisco.

'Carlos doesn't know that I'm sitting for you, Senor Fernandez. Please, please don't tell him. He'll be so angry with me if he finds out.' She twisted her hands in anguish. 'But my mother is so ill and we can't afford the doctor's bills. The money you pay me is not much, but it does help.'

'My dear Mercedes, please don't distress yourself.' Francisco told her everything that had happened. Finally he said, 'So you see we now have to find some way of persuading Carlos to allow Conchita and me to marry, without letting him find out that you've been posing for me.' He looked at them both anxiously.

Conchita sat in an agony of suspense. She could see no way out of their dilemma. 'Francisco, Carlos has some loyal friends, and they…'

'Shhh… please Conchita.' Francisco was silent for a few moments, while he paced around the studio. 'Ah I have it, and I hope this will work.' He turned to Mercedes. 'The portrait I'm painting of you is only my first attempt at the nude form, and at present it's not going too well, so I'm prepared to put all thoughts of painting in this form out of my mind. I'm not a poor man, as my father left me well provided for, and I have several other assignments waiting to be completed, including the one I'm doing with Conchita.'

Mercedes put her head in her hands, and after a few moments, she looked up again. 'Thank you Senor Fernandez, but I don't know how I'll be able to manage without this money. I won't be able to pay the bills, and my mother will…'

Large tears began to fall down her cheeks, and Conchita's heart went out to her.

Francisco looked troubled as he turned to Mercedes. 'Will you be seeing Carlos this evening?'

'Yes,' she said, looking fearful and bewildered.

'Then that's good. This is what you must tell him…'

Conchita's heart pounded, as she listened to his words.

The hot sun was streaming mercilessly through Conchita's narrow bedroom window when she woke from yet another troubled night's sleep. She could already hear the sound of a dog barking and the clip-clop sound of a donkey as it made its weary way along the street below her window. Her first thought was of Francisco and how much she loved him: her second thought was about Mercedes, and whether their plan had worked.

She walked downstairs and was immediately confronted by Carlos, but for once, he had a broad smile on his face.

'Conchita, I…'

'Yes, Carlos.'

'It would seem that I've misjudged your Senor Fernandez.'

'Yes, I think you have,' she replied, trying to look and sound innocent.

'Unfortunately, my dear friend Mercedes is distressed as her mother is sick, and needs urgent medical care. The family is having great difficulty paying the doctor's bills and this has been worrying me too, because I'm not able to help her myself.' Carlos looked almost embarrassed as he continued. 'You may have noticed that I've been going out with Mercedes recently. She told me that Jose, a mutual friend of ours, introduced her to Senor Fernandez, ostensibly to discuss her mother's illness. Apparently Francisco is quite a rich man.' Carlos smiled. 'As a result, he's offered to pay all her doctor's bills. My animosity towards him has gone. He is a generous man, Conchita, and I applaud him.' He smiled again, and cleared his throat. 'I feel I may have acted rather too hastily in saying that you shouldn't marry him,' he said looking down his nose at her. 'I've heard that his father was a great benefactor and extremely wealthy. In fact he owned the Artists' House, and it all now belongs to Francisco. I've also heard that the various rumours about his lifestyle, are totally untrue, and caused by jealousy. Francisco is obviously following in his father's footsteps, as he often helped people financially whilst he was alive; a trait which seems to run in the family. So in the circumstances, how could I stop you from marrying him?'

'Carlos, thank you. You don't know how happy your words have made me,' she said, reaching up to plant a gentle kiss on his forehead.

Carlos smiled again. 'I've learned an important lesson, Conchita. All this has made me realise that gossip, and rumours, can be enormously destructive.' He brushed his long curly hair away from his eyes. 'There's one other thing. I made a few enquiries last night. It would appear that the stories about Francisco starting to use nude models are also untrue. A case of jealousy again, I suspect. I will visit him this morning to apologise, and tell him that I believe him to be a fit and honest man who will be able to look after you properly.'

'Yes, he is. I have always known so. Thank you Carlos.' She smiled. Her brother had always respected, and looked up to people who had plenty of money, so Conchita felt slightly ashamed of her part in this deception, but not for long, as everybody was now so happy. She could hardly wait to see Francisco again, but before that, she had her duties to perform. Conchita had promised her father whilst he was on his death-bed, that she would be her brothers' little mother until such time as they no longer needed her. Pablo was soon to be married, and she believed that if Mercedes had her way, Carlos would not be far behind.

'Well my little sister, are you going to cook us some breakfast or not?'

'Yes of course, Carlos,' she answered, her eyes flashing with hidden triumph.

THE VILLAGE FETE

The morning of the Steeple Norford Annual Village Fete, being held on the green that afternoon, dawned miserably. The sky was dark, the clouds were moving quickly across the sky, and there seemed little chance of any improvement in the weather. The persistent rain slanted down upon the colourful marquees and stalls, which were dotted haphazardly around the green. The Union Jacks and gaily coloured bunting hung with care the day before, now dripped sorrowfully in sodden strands, and were too heavy to be moved much by the prevailing south-westerly breeze.

Elderly, frail widow, Agnes Watson looked at the scene set out before her from the downstairs bedroom window of her beautiful little rose-covered thatched house known locally as Lilac Cottage. An old, but beautiful lilac tree stood proudly just to the left of the entrance gate. Her garden was always well looked after, and crammed full of her favourite flowers. But today Agnes felt sad, because the bad weather had flattened some of them and they were now lying flat on the ground. 'Oh how I wish it would stop raining,' she said. She smiled when she saw her neighbour, Ned Beckington working hard as usual. As her garden was quite small, he regarded it almost as an extension of his own, and tended it with all the loving care that Agnes could no longer bestow upon it. Ned was smiling as he looked up at the lowering sky. She loved the way he always wore his old straw hat perched cheekily on the back of his head, and didn't seem to mind the rainwater streaming into his eyes. Agnes knew that Ned enjoyed this kind of weather, as he'd told her that it made all the plants grow bigger and stronger.

Day after day Agnes, who was unable to walk far, would sit in front of the window to watch the comings and goings of the people of Steeple Norford. When Ned saw her sitting in her usual place, he waved. She could just make out his call of 'Mornin' Mrs. Watson, and how are you today?' Agnes waved back with as much enthusiasm as she could muster, due to the pain from her increasingly painful arthritic joints.

The day of the village fete was always special for Agnes, as it brought back so many precious memories of her husband... her darling Charles. She couldn't help wondering if today would be the day when she would see him again, but with her ageing eyesight would she be able to pick him out of the crowd, and would he rush into her army and call her "a silly goose", just like he used to? But deep down, Agnes knew she was being foolish, because he'd been dead for so many long years.

Agnes watched as a group of people all laughing and talking happily, arrived on the green. They carried baskets filled to the brim with rolled-up coloured paper, tablecloths, balloons, and everything else needed to help make their particular stall look more appealing. Some carried pretty patterned umbrellas to protect them from the rain, and they contributed to the gaiety of the day. Others were weighed down as they carried chairs, bunting, notice boards, and placards which were all essential ingredients to help to make the Fete a financial success.

Two middle-aged women, who were staggering along with a load of cakes and buns, made their way over to the cake stall. Agnes could see them laughing excitedly. Then she saw a young woman in a beautiful red dress with a full skirt. She was trying to carry a huge box of bric-a-brac items, which were obviously destined for the white-elephant stall. Despite being in pain, Agnes couldn't help smiling. 'Why should a stall selling anything antique or old, be given the name of a "White Elephant Stall"? Perhaps I'd be considered to be a White Elephant myself now, because I'm so old,' she said.

Agnes's happy mood soon faded. Her cushions were old too, and she suddenly felt uncomfortable. She wriggled in her seat as more old memories flooded into her tired brain. She continued to watch the girl wearing the red dress, as it reminded her of the one she'd worn so many years before. 'I wonder if she's looking for someone she loves too? Oh dear…'

Uncontrolled tears fell down her cheeks as she remembered the intense love she felt for Charles, until she realised the utter futility of it all. 'Stop it, you silly old woman,' she told herself, as she released the painful memory from her mind.

Agnes could see the various stallholders and helpers all chatting away in animated conversation as they went about their tasks. They all seemed convinced that the weather forecast would be correct. The incessant rain would gradually disappear, and allow the sun to come shining through. She fidgeted in her chair again, trying to make herself more comfortable. All she could do now was just sit and watch the world go by without her. 'How I long to go out into the fresh air, feel the wind in my hair, and be able to walk around the green, hand-in-hand with Charles, once more,' she said. 'Yes, I do know this is impossible. I'm just a silly tired old woman who has nothing better to do, but talk to herself.'

Steeple Norford nestled proudly amidst the rolling hills of Sussex, in southern England, as it had done for hundreds of years. The population consisted mainly of local tradespeople, a few commuters, farmers and their workers, and had remained reasonably static over the years. Some of the more affluent inhabitants had moved away and on to better things, or so they thought. Yet others from afar only took one look at the village to declare that they could never ever live anywhere else. But strangely, its character had remained roughly the same.

The representatives of the various organisations in and around the village met annually to arrange the fete. This year the day chosen just happened to coincide with the 70th Anniversary of V.E. Day, which was a most important event in the village, and the country. After much squabbling about what form the celebrations should take, the organising committee eventually agreed, and they'd all rushed away eager to put their plans into action.

The fete had been held on the same spot for nearly two hundred years, and the proceeds were always given to the St. James's Church Restoration Fund. The ancient church was situated at the far end of the green. Agnes screwed her eyes up, and adjusted her glasses in order to see it more clearly. The spire was still twisted and hadn't changed at all over these long and lonely years, she thought sadly. Her grey, watery, myopic eyes suddenly grew tired and misty. She sighed and yet despite her earlier reluctance, she began to recall the day so long ago when her love for Charles had first blossomed…

It was 1938 on a balmy summer's day, and nineteen year old Agnes, was preparing to meet Charles. He was in the army, and she had walked out with him several times recently. 'He's so upright and handsome,' she said, as she pirouetted happily in front of the mirror, making her favourite red silk dress swirl around her long, slim legs. She placed two pretty tortoiseshell combs into her Veronica Lake-style blond hair, and feeling satisfied with her appearance, looked eagerly out of the window once more to see if she could see him. Her excitement was heightened as each minute passed by. 'Charles is so patient, kind and wonderful,' she said, feeling the first stirrings of real love igniting within her.

There wasn't a cloud in the sky on that particular day, and people were already out on the village green preparing for the grand opening of the fete. Agnes felt unusually elated and excited, as though something really wonderful was about to happen. Then she saw Charles striding quickly across the green, and her eyes followed him as he bent down to open the low white, wooden gate. Agnes waited for her mother to answer the door, and when she heard the sound of his voice, her heart fluttered with excitement. She quickly patted her hair, checked her appearance once again, and twirled round in front of the full length mirror again, before walking out of her bedroom.

Charles greeted her with great affection. 'Hello, my dearest Aggie,' he'd said looking at her with love in his eyes. 'You look absolutely wonderful.' In turn, she remembered thinking how dashing he looked in his uniform. He was such an upstanding and handsome young man, and her heart melted. His military-type moustache always seemed to turn up at the edges, and Agnes supposed this was because he was always smiling and laughing.

Later, they strolled hand in hand around the green, both quite unaware of what was going on around them; they could have been anywhere. They didn't see the milling, happy crowds of people throwing wooden balls at coconuts which were too firmly placed in their holders. They didn't hear the excitement when someone managed to throw a ring around a hoped for prize, or smell the delicious aroma of the food on offer in the tea tent. The races went on in the centre of the green as they sauntered by, and even the noisy crowd, which had gathered around the amateur boxing ring, failed to gain their attention. None of these things even

37

existed for either of them. They were cocooned in a little place of their own, and nothing could encroach upon their happiness.

Soon after passing the coconut shy for the second time, Charles stopped, smiled, and looked down at her. He took her small hands tenderly into his, and with his voice filled with emotion, he whispered, 'My darling Aggie, I have something important to say to you.'

'Yes, Charles,' she answered, her heart thumping away in her chest. She thought that he'd never looked quite so wonderful before. His eyes sparkled, and she felt that she could plunge into their depths and... remain there forever.

'Well, firstly, I would like to tell you how much I love you, my darling Aggie,' he said. 'I know we're in the middle of the village green, and I shouldn't make an absolute fool of myself by getting down on one knee to propose to you in front of all these people, but I feel that I should.' Charles immediately ignored anyone walking by and knelt down in front of her. 'I would be honoured if you would consent to become my wife.' Agnes giggled. 'Secondly, I am being sent away for a while.' The last few words were said almost as an aside. Agnes opened her mouth to say something, but Charles was in full flow. 'So perhaps we could get married during my next leave? You will wait for me, won't you, my dearest girl?' he said, his eyes searching hers for the answer he needed.

'Oh my darling Charles,' she answered breathlessly. 'I love you so much, and of course I will marry you. I will wait for you forever, if necessary.'

'My dear Aggie, as you know, I'm never quite sure how long I'll be away.' He bent down and kissed her gently on the lips. 'There that seals it. You've made me the happiest man in the world.'

Agnes looked up at him in wonderment. Their kiss felt

like every pleasant sensation she had ever known, and her words tumbled out in a rush.

'Oh Charles, thank you and I mean... Oh I don't know what I mean, but you've made me the happiest woman in the world,' she replied, her heart full of joy. Her elation quickly disappeared when she remembered what he'd said before he'd kissed her. She couldn't help feeling anxious and fearful for his safety. 'Charles, you said just now that you are going away for a while. Where are they are sending you?'

He took hold of both her hands again. 'Don't look so worried Aggie darling. They're making arrangements to send me to Berlin, but I'm not quite sure when.'

'Berlin! But Charles won't that be dangerous? I've heard so many stories about what is going on out there, and...'

'I really have no choice in the matter, my darling girl. I have already received my orders.' He lifted her chin upwards. 'You silly little goose, everything will be alright, you'll see.'

From that moment on, Agnes lost her heart completely, and forever.

Three weeks later, Charles came home on leave and managed to obtain a special marriage licence despite opposition from her parents. They regarded the young couple's decision to get married to be too soon.

'Agnes,' her father had said, 'My dear girl, you are still very young. Are you sure that you know what you are doing? Charles seems a nice enough chap, but you hardly know one another do you?'

Agnes refused to listen to his worries. 'Daddy, of course we know what we're doing. There's probably going to be a war soon, and who knows what's going to happen? We feel there's no point in waiting.'

39

They were married in the local church in front of their families and friends. The sun shone down upon them, making them feel blessed and blissfully happy. But this feeling was short-lived however, as a month after their wedding, Charles was posted to Berlin. For a while, Charles was able to return to England on leave, but once war with Germany was declared, he found it impossible to get out of the city.

It was several weeks before Agnes heard from the War Office that Charles had been killed during a disturbance involving several members of the growing Hitler Youth Movement. He'd simply been in the wrong place at the wrong time. Agnes thought the end of the world had arrived. She was heartbroken, and lost interest in everything that went on around her.

The years rolled slowly by, and Agnes waited for Charles. Every year since then on the day of the village fete, Agnes would watch and eagerly wait, hoping that she would see his happy, smiling face in the crowd, so that she could once again walk around the green with him.

With some difficulty, Agnes pulled herself away from the wonderful, but sad memories of the past, as this year's Anniversary Fete was now in full swing.

A group of about six war veterans, each wearing their uniforms and medals with immense pride, were preparing to march around the village green. As if on cue, the rain which had been falling for several hours, suddenly stopped and the sun came out. Agnes stared at the war veterans, and tears began to form in her eyes. They had all survived that dreadful war, but Charles didn't, she thought miserably, as her mind began to wander again.

She had forgotten a lot of things in her life since that time, but never how wonderful Charles looked in his uniform, as they sauntered around the green together. He'd just proposed to her, and she'd accepted. She remembered feeling so happy at the time, and everything was right with her world.

But, she'd never forgotten her promise to him that she would wait for him for ever. Agnes's eyesight was now hazy, and her body was frail, but her memory was still clear. She'd never married again, believing that no man could ever take Charles' place in her heart. She remembered so clearly as if it was only yesterday, when Charles had said goodbye to her, and later when she'd learned of his untimely death. It was forever etched in her memory.

The warmth of the sun soon penetrated through her bedroom window, and Agnes was once again brought painfully back to the present. 'If only… if only. How I wish I could see you again, Charles,' she said. Unrestrained tears began to fall down her face, and dropped unnoticed into her lap.

Agnes felt a strange weakness pass over her, which was something she'd experienced a few times lately. She'd been unable to eat or sleep properly over the last few days, and she sighed. She was old, and felt tired of life itself, and as she looked out of the window she somehow seemed to know that it would be for the last time.

She watched as the group of old servicemen slowly disappeared into the tea tent. Some young people wearing red, white and blue clothing, and waving Union Jacks, sauntered around the green together. Her window was open, and somewhere a band was playing. Then she heard some people singing *"We'll meet again"*, and tears once again fell slowly down her cheeks.

Agnes closed her eyes.

Suddenly she saw Charles. He was wearing his uniform, and waving as he walked towards her. He looked so

41

handsome and dapper. 'Oh my dearest Charles,' she said as her frail heart fluttered. 'I've been waiting... I knew you would come back for me. What kept you?'

Agnes took a long, and lingering deep breath...

The milkman discovered Agnes the following morning. He'd been unable to rouse her and had looked in through the window. She was sitting bolt upright in her chair, with her dead sightless eyes still staring out towards the village green...

...and she was smiling so happily.

MISTER SMILIE

The news reader looked grim as he started to read the latest bulletin. *"Yet another bomb has exploded in the city of..."* Jo turned the television off. 'Oh, not again,' she said in despair. 'When is it ever going to end?' Even though she was still only a teenager, she really cared about what was going on. It was all so depressing. and she knew there was nothing she could do about it.

Jo plumped up the cushions on the settee, and noticed with dismay, that despite her mother's efforts to keep everything looking well cared for, another large, frayed hole had appeared in the old fragile flowered material. She knew her parents couldn't afford to buy any new furniture because times were hard. She sighed. 'They deserve better than this,' she said to herself sadly. She was aware that Christmas Day was only two weeks' away, so she decided to search through all the old Christmas decorations to see if any of them were worth using again.

'Oh dear,' she sighed. 'They've all been used for such a long time' Jo picked up an old, but still pretty, golden star, and turned it round and round in her hands. She remembered making it at school about seven years ago and she'd felt really proud when her father had placed it on top of the Christmas tree. She gave a wry smile as some of the glitter sparkled briefly, before falling to the floor. 'There's hardly any left now,' she said, placing it back in the box.

Jo felt really sad, as she knew that it would be a frugal Christmas this year, because everything was so expensive. It would be wonderful if Dad could get a proper job, she thought as she looked around the room again. She paused, closed her eyes and whispered quietly... I wish, I wish... Oh how I wish.'

A sudden noise outside made her jump; it sounded like

a cat yowling. She pulled the old faded curtains to one side, and peered through the misty window. 'Oh, it's been snowing,' she said with delight. The full moon cast its magical, silvery light on to everything, making quite ordinary things seem special. The small plain terraced houses huddled together under a cold blanket of snow, and the parked cars outside each wore a white covering like the icing on a cake. Even the garden path showed no sign that its surface was pitted and uneven.

It was then that Jo noticed the tiny footprints in the snow. Starting from the gate, they came up to the porch, turned round in an arc, and then retreated to the gate once more. Her fascinated gaze took in the snowy contours of the top of the gate, and then on to the brick wall. A beautiful black cat was sitting with its long tail wrapped around its feet in a classic pose. Jo frowned as it seemed to be staring at the house, and she wondered what it wanted; perhaps it's hungry, she thought.

Jo had just celebrated her seventeenth birthday, and was feeling a little lonely now that the term at the local sixth-form college had ended. She'd finished her holiday study period for her exams, and her older brother Chris, had not yet come home from work. Unfortunately, both her parents were away. Her mother was looking after Jo's grandmother who was ill. Her father, an out of work architect, was offered the chance of doing some voluntary work in a town several miles away, and this necessitated him staying there for a few days. The job entailed helping to design and build a new Community Centre for elderly people. Even though he had little or no money, he was giving his time and expertise for next to nothing. The fact that he wasn't able to contribute much to the family's income didn't occur to him, but nevertheless they were all proud of him.

Jo continued to watch the cat. Suddenly, it jumped off the wall, walked up to the porch, and sat down on the doorstep. 'I'm sure it's the same cat I saw in the garden the day Dad went away. It must be homeless and so cold, poor little thing.' Without thinking, she raced to the front door, opened it… and the cat simply walked in. He looked up at Jo with his green appealing eyes before curling and twisting himself around her legs. He then made his way along the hallway, and into the family's living room. Jo was amazed; he seemed to know the way!

Jo had lit the fire earlier, and the room felt warm and welcoming. The cat sat down on the old rug in front of the fireplace, and peered into the depths of the dancing flames. Then to her surprise, he turned his head, and… seemed to smile at her. Tears formed in Jo's eyes as she looked at him. His fur was black, apart from a small patch of heart-shaped white fur underneath his chin. 'Oh, you are so beautiful,' she said when she noticed a few stray white hairs on each dainty little foot, and the way his coat shone with a curious blue sheen. All this was accentuated by the glow from the fire. He purred loudly, and Jo couldn't resist stroking him. Afterwards, he stretched himself out on the rug with a self-satisfied look on his handsome face.

'Well now you're here, I suppose you would like some milk?' Jo said, once again stroking him. She stood up, walked into the kitchen, found a little stainless steel bowl, filled it with milk and placed it on the floor. When she opened the fridge to put the milk away, one of the plastic shelves broke as it clattered onto the floor. She shook her head: the fridge and the cooker both need replacing, but when will we ever have enough money to buy new ones, she wondered. Jo's eyes brimmed with tears as she repeated her three wishes… 'I wish… I wish… I wish.' She felt sorry for her parents, and wanted to help them in some way, so she decided to talk to them both about whether she could get some part-time work after Christmas.

She was about to return to the living room, when she heard the sound of a key being inserted in the front door. It was her brother Chris, and he called out as he entered the house.

'Hello, Jo. It's only me.'

'Hi Chris,' she said walking out into the hall and wondering what on earth she could say about their surprise visitor?

'Wow, it's freezing out there' he said rubbing his hands together. 'Have you lit the fire yet? If not, I'll do it for you.' He walked straight into the living room, and stopped short when he saw the cat lying sprawled out on the rug in front of the fire. 'Hello, who are you?' he said, 'and what are you doing in here?'

Jo stood in the doorway. 'I've no idea who he belongs to, Chris. I opened the front door, and he just walked in. I didn't have the heart to put him out in the snow again.'

The cat turned his head, smiled, stood up and stretched, before walking out of the room to look for the milk he seemed to know Jo had left for him. She followed him into the kitchen, her forehead creased with unanswered questions. She watched as the cat lapped the milk up daintily, and followed him as he returned to his spot in front of the fire. By now she was fascinated by this feline stranger. His gaze was intense, and she felt that he was trying to tell her something. They were surrounded in silence for a few moments, apart from the slight hiss, and the odd crackle from the logs in the grate.

And the cat continued to stare.

'Chris, I want to keep him,' she found herself compelled to say.

'Keep him?'

'Yes.'

'Keeping a cat costs money, Jo. It'll be another mouth for Mum and Dad to feed,' he said. 'There will be vet's fees and...'

46

'I know all that, but...' she hesitated. 'It suddenly seems important for us to keep him. I can't explain... something is telling me... almost insisting that we keep him.' She looked at her brother, smiled...

...and the cat did the same.

'But Jo, supposing he already has a home? Perhaps he was just cold and needed a drink?'

'Well, if he does have a home somewhere, we'll have to give him up,' she replied quietly.

Over the next few days, Jo made several enquiries, but nobody seemed to know anything about him. As for the cat, he simply sat on the rug in front of the fire and made himself at home. Jo and Chris decided to call him 'Mr. Smilie', because that's what he did most of the time.

The next day, two letters arrived. One was from her father, as she recognised his writing, and the other one looked important, so she put it to one side. When she opened the letter from her father, happy tears began to form in Jo's eyes, and she looked down at Mr. Smilie.

'Dad's coming home tomorrow, and you'll be able to meet him. Oh I can't wait. I've got so much to tell him.' She stared at the official-looking envelope on the table. 'What I wouldn't give for this letter to be good news, Mr. Smilie,' she said suddenly feeling tearful. His slanting green eyes seemed to fill with compassionate understanding. He purred loudly in apparent agreement, and once again Jo had the feeling it would bring good news for them all.

The following evening the snow had begun to thaw and she was looking out of the window to see if she could see her father walking towards the house. He always had a spring in his step, but lately he seemed to have all the world's problems upon his broad shoulders.

Mr. Smilie sat beside her on the windowsill as if he too, was anxious to see him.

When her father at last arrived home, Jo stood on the doorstep with the white envelope in her hand.

'Hello, my darling Jo. I'm so glad to be home again,' he said. She handed him the envelope. He glanced at it, wiped his feet on the doormat and said, 'Let me get in first please Jo, and then I'll open it. It's probably only another bill, and I already have a pile of those waiting for me. Perhaps you could put the kettle on for a cup of tea, please?' He sighed. 'Sorry love, I'm feeling really tired.'

Once Jo had made the tea, her father sat at the kitchen table and stared at the envelope, but he still didn't open it. 'Jo, I've missed you both so much, and I can't wait for your mother to come home. I'm so sorry that I can't provide you all with a decent home, good food and... what with Christmas coming soon, I...'

'Dad, please open your letter? It... it might be good news.'

'Good news! I wish...' He picked the envelope up, and Jo could see his hands were shaking.

'Open it, Dad, please.'

'O.K... O.K... I'll open it, if it will keep you quiet.' With shaking hands, he tore at the envelope, and withdrew a single sheet of paper. As he read the letter his whole demeanour began to change. He smiled... and then he laughed.

'What is it, Dad?'

'Jo, I've been offered a job at last. Do you remember the interview I had a few weeks' ago? As I hadn't heard anything I assumed that I wasn't successful. But I was, and I'll be earning more money... a lot more money. I can't believe it after all this time.' Tears filled his eyes and he brushed them away. 'Wow... Jo they want me to start in the New Year. I can't wait to tell your mother.' He stood up, strode into the sitting room, and flopped down in his favourite chair beside the fire.

It was then that he noticed Mr. Smilie sitting on the rug by the fire.

'Jo. What's this cat doing here?'

'Dad, he first appeared the day you went away. I know it sounds silly, but deep down I feel it's important that we give him a home. Please say we can?'

Jo, and Mr. Smilie both looked at him and... held their breath.

'I don't think...' The cat continued to stare. 'Well... well I suppose we can let him stay, providing of course that your mother agrees.' The cat turned his head back towards the fire with a look of triumph on his face. A few seconds later they heard the phone ringing in the hall, and Jo raced to answer it.

'Jo, it's Mum here. Grandma is so much better. In fact if everyone agrees, I'll be bringing her back here, so that we can all celebrate Christmas together. Isn't it great?'

'Mum that's wonderful news. I can't wait to see you both,' Jo said happily. 'We have some surprises for you too. The most important one is that Dad's just come home.' Jo felt so happy that she thought her heart would burst. Suddenly everything seemed to be going right.

Even her mother sounded more positive. 'There are one or two arrangements I'll have to make Jo darling, but we should be home tomorrow afternoon. Then we can start thinking about Christmas.'

'Oh Mum, I'm so happy,' Jo said, as tears began to flow down her face. 'I can't wait.'

The following evening the whole family sat together in the living room, hardly believing their good fortune. Jo's father stood up with a glass in his hands, and smiled for the first time in ages.

'Well everyone, cheers. What a homecoming,' he said.

'I can't believe what's happened since I went away.' He looked around at his family; they were all laughing and smiling happily. 'A black cat is supposed to bring good luck, and he certainly appeared at the right time. I think we should welcome Mr. Smilie into our family.'

Jo was overjoyed. 'Thank you, Dad.'

Mr. Smiled had trudged through the snow, leaving a little trail of footprints behind him, and had stopped at their house. He couldn't have brought a better Christmas present for the family either. A kind of magical happiness had descended upon them, which filled their hearts with happiness, and hope for the future.

Had there been magic in the air, or was Mr. Smilie just looking for a home?

Only he knew the answer, and he sat listening to their excited happy voices. He looked at each member of his new family in turn. He knew that his life, and theirs, were now inextricably joined.

Mr. Smilie turned his face towards the fire…

…and how he smiled.

THE UNINVITED

A small crowd of mourners stood sombrely around a graveside on a chilly, summer's afternoon. A veil of light rain added to the mood of deep sorrow. The area around the freshly prepared grave was beautiful, with tall proud oak trees standing like sentinels around this quiet, shady spot. It was considered to be the perfect last resting place for the deceased.

The vicar, The Reverend Brian Anderson, was part of the way through the committal proceedings, and now and again his words were whipped away by the freshening wind.

'Man that was born of woman has but...'

Molly Jenkinson was trying hard to concentrate on what he was saying, when her attention was caught by a sudden movement in her line of vision. She nudged her boyfriend.

'Adam, did you notice a woman standing over there by those old oak trees, just now? She's definitely hiding,' she whispered, covering her mouth with a delicately manicured hand.

'No, I didn't see anything. It was probably your imagination. Perhaps it was a bird or an animal,' he replied. 'Anyway, I'm trying to listen to the committal service, Molly.'

'But... Adam, I...'

'Please be quiet. This is a funeral, remember?'

'Sorry,' Molly said, whilst looking back over her shoulder.

The vicar continued in his deep sonorous voice, '...dust to dust, ashes to ashes...' Another gust of wind sent his words drifting off into the ether. Molly hadn't known the man who was being buried today very well as she'd only met him a couple of times. His name was John Armitage and he was Adam's cousin. John had been mad about anything to do with fast cars, and this obsession eventually lead to his downfall; he was killed in a car accident on the motorway a few days earlier. Molly couldn't help thinking that if she'd known Adam and his family a little better, her concentration would not have begun to waver.

Another slight movement again drew her attention away from the graveside. Her forehead creased as she concentrated on one oak tree in particular. 'Yes,' she whispered. 'Look Adam, there is someone standing behind that tree, and if they don't wish to be seen, then they're not making a very good job of it.' Molly could clearly see a shapely female leg, wearing an extremely high-heeled shoe, and a short black skirt. 'I wonder who she is, and more to the point, why didn't she want anyone to know she's here?' Adam glared at her, and then looked away. She tried to concentrate on the committal proceedings, but it was impossible; He was ignoring her, but she had to say something. 'Adam, there has to be some reason why this woman is hiding. I wonder if John had been having an affair!'

When he still didn't answer, she frowned. In some ways he and his moods were unreadable. She began to wonder why he was being so short with her? Was it because he's upset that his cousin has died, or perhaps the whole family is such a tightly controlled unit, that they're reluctant to accept strangers into their midst? Adam's family had been sort of welcoming to her, but there was a slight reticence about getting to know her, and this was starting to worry Molly.

About five minutes later, the committal service ended, and the mourners began to walk back along the path towards the car park. Molly stood for a moment to see if she could see the woman again, but whoever she was, she was being a little more careful.

Adam turned to her impatiently, 'Come along, Molly we have to go. This rain is getting heavier by the minute. We must get back to the house to help Anna serve the food and drinks. If you remember, we promised we would help her,' he said haughtily.

'Yes, of course I remember, but can we wait a few minutes more, please Adam? This could be really important, for Anna,' she whispered. 'There's a woman over there. Who is she, and why is she hiding behind that tree?' Molly pushed a few sodden strands of her long dark hair out of her eyes. 'Let's move over there for a moment,' she said practically dragging Adam over to a large obelisk-shaped gravestone, nearer to the tree.

'Molly please, for goodness sake, we have to go now.'

'Shhh,' she said, 'she might hear you.'

'But...'

'Shhh...'

They stood behind the gravestone in silence for a while, until the rest of the mourners had drifted away. Molly, being of an inquisitive nature, looked round the edge of the stone. To her surprise, a tall, elegant woman dressed completely in black, and wearing a veiled hat of truly Ascot proportions, emerged from behind the oak tree.

'Look Adam,' she said. 'I told you there was someone there, but you wouldn't listen. And she's carrying some flowers.' After looking around, the woman walked hesitantly over to the open grave, and threw them on top of the coffin. She stood for a few moments looking downwards, before lifting her black veil, and holding a handkerchief up to her nose.

'Adam,' Molly whispered excitedly. 'Who is she?' The

woman was beautiful, and she looked at her with admiration.

Adam didn't reply, but he stared at her with a frown upon his face. 'I'm not sure, but she looks a little like… Oh my God…!'

'What's the matter? Do you know her then?'

'Yes, I most certainly do know her, the bi… This is really going to upset the family. I can't believe it!'

'What do you mean?' Molly said pulling a face. 'Come on Adam; please don't get all mysterious on me. Who is she?'

'Shhh, she's going. I'll tell you in a minute.' They watched as the woman stumbled up the gravelled pathway towards the old wooden gate. She turned round to take a last look at the grave, before walking through the gate. 'She's… I don't know how to say this.' He hesitated. 'She's John's wife… er, I mean widow, and her name is Heather. I knew who she was as soon as she lifted the veil. You don't forget a face like hers in a hurry, believe me, or the woman behind it,' he added bitterly.

'John's widow! You didn't tell me he was married. I naturally assumed that he was single. I heard a man talking to Anna after you'd introduced me a few weeks ago, and he mentioned something about them getting engaged. Anna was rather non-committal at the time, and I wondered why? Wow!'

'Well now you know the reason why I didn't tell you,' he replied tersely. Water was dripping down his neck from a ledge high up on the gravestone, and he pulled up the collar of his overcoat. 'John married Heather over ten years ago, but it didn't last. Within three years it was all over. After that, she left the country and nobody seems to have heard anything more about her. Fancy her turning up like this. How dare she?' Adam was quiet for a moment, and Molly could see he was seething. 'Do you know, I bet she heard about John's death and came back to England to hear the reading of the will? It's on Tuesday morning by the way. It's just the kind of thing she would do. The whole family is convinced that she's a money grabber.' Adam, looked at Molly. 'I wonder if John changed his will?'

'Poor Anna! If he hasn't, would this mean that his widow, Heather, could inherit the whole estate?' she said in reply.

Adam's face wore a look of confused anger. 'It certainly looks like it. Damn it. Everyone knows that John was a rich man. Even the four cars in his garage are worth a fortune. What on earth am I going to say to Anna? If Heather turns up at the will reading as well, it will cause absolute havoc.'

'Did Anna know that he was still married to Heather? I hope she did.'

'I have absolutely no idea.' Adam closed his eyes in anguish, 'All I know is that I have to tell Anna that Heather is here, and it's the last thing she needs at a time like this.'

'Sooner you than me,' she said planting a sudden kiss on his cheek. 'It's a good job I persuaded you to stay a little longer. Come on let's go, we're getting soaked.'

'We can go now, can we?' Adam said.

They were the last to arrive at Anna's house for the after-funeral tea. They rang the bell and her tear-stained face peered around the door.

'There you are,' Anna said. 'I was wondering what had happened to both of you. You said you were going to help. Anyway, come on in and take those wet coats off. Everyone's waiting, so go straight into the sitting room.'

Adam seemed agitated as they took off their wet coats.

Finally with a look of hopelessness on his face, he turned to Molly. 'Will you tell her, or shall I?'

Molly began to panic. 'Adam, John was your cousin, not mine. I'm not a member of the family, and I don't think Anna would take too kindly to me telling her something like that. It has to come from you,' she replied.

'Yes, of course. But I don't know what to say to her.'

'All you need to say is that you saw Heather at the cemetery and then wait for her to question you about what happened.'

'Mmm, that sounds like a good idea. I'll try that.' Adam sighed deeply. 'But could you perhaps clear the way for me, by telling Anna that I need to speak to her in the kitchen then, please?'

'Oh Adam, do I have to, only I…?'

'It's not too much to ask, is it?' he said with his face a thunderous mask. He turned away from her, and walked towards the kitchen.

Molly was a little stung by Adam's reaction, and entered the crowded, noisy sitting room, feeling cross that she had to be the one to speak to Anna, when she didn't know or recognise anyone. Everyone seemed to be talking at once, mostly about John, drinking tea and eating sandwiches. So where was Anna?

Molly eventually found her sitting on a sofa and speaking to an older woman. She took a deep breath and approached them. 'I'm really sorry to interrupt you Anna, but Adam would like to speak to you about… about something that happened at the cemetery this afternoon. It's rather important, and he's waiting for you in the kitchen.'

'Is that why you were both so late getting here, then?' Anna replied. 'Help yourself to a cup of tea.' She walked quickly out of the room, and Molly winced as she heard the kitchen door close with a thump. She sat in the corner of the room drinking her tea, and not one person bothered to speak to her, and she began to wonder if even Adam had forgotten about her. Doubts about her relationship with him began to swirl around in her brain... and they gradually began to surface.

It was just before ten o'clock on a dreary, blustery Tuesday morning. The Armitage family and close friends, made their way to the offices of Messrs. Parker, Parker and Hind. They were shown into a sumptuous, book-lined room to await the arrival of the solicitor who would be reading the Last Will and Testament of the deceased, John Henry Armitage.

A door opened, and Mr. Joseph Parker the senior partner entered the room, walked over to his desk and picked up the relevant file. He stopped to look at all the people gathered before him, cleared his throat, and began to speak.

'Firstly, I would like to say good morning to you all, and thank you for coming. The reading of a will is always a sad occasion. Would you all be seated please?' He looked carefully around the room before speaking again. 'I'm afraid that we must wait for one more person to arrive before I can begin to read John's Last Will and Testament. I...'

At that moment, the door opened and a woman walked into the room.

An audible gasp, quickly followed by an embarrassing silence, greeted her arrival.

Heather Armitage smiled and looked at everyone before saying in a slight American accent, 'I'm so sorry I'm a little late, and I do apologise if I kept you all waiting.' Her smile soon faded as she walked to the back of the room, and sat down on the only empty chair available.

Molly looked at Anna to see how she reacted, but her face was an emotionless mask, as she stared straight ahead.

'Right, if we are all ready, I will begin,' Joseph Parker announced pompously. 'This is the Last Will and Testament of the deceased, John Henry Armitage and it is dated... the 3rd of January in the year... 2008.' He emphasised the date, and looked around the room to see if there were any objections. 'I have to tell you that there have been no changes to this Will since that date.'

Anna's distressed voice rang out, interrupting the proceedings. 'My God, that was nine years ago... John didn't change his Will. I don't believe it. How could he have done this, after promising us faithfully that he would?' She burst into tears.

Joseph Parker looked up, but was in no way deterred from his task, and continued to read out the details of a few small bequests. Finally he read, 'I leave the main part of my estate, shares and any accrued interest to my wife, Heather.'

This was all too much for Anna. She stood up and walked over to where Heather was sitting. 'I know you are still legally his widow, but you've had nothing to do with John over the last few years, and you've got the nerve to come back here expecting to inherit all his money. What about the rest of the family? How can you sleep at night? Have you no shame?' Anna turned away too shocked to say anymore. There was a hushed silence as she returned to her seat.

Heather Armitage, looking elegantly beautiful in an expensive designer suit, stood up and walked towards the solicitor's desk, before turning round to face her deceased husband's family. All eyes were immediately focused upon her, and then everyone began to speak at once.

'Please would you all be quiet for a moment,' she said raising her voice. 'I know what you have all been thinking, but you're wrong… in fact you are very wrong. I came over here from America to pay my last respects to my husband, John.' Her statement was met with a stunned silence.

Molly squeezed Adam's arm and whispered, 'Surely she's entitled to, isn't she?'

'For God's sake not now, Molly please! Your timing is perfect, as always,' he snapped with more than a hint of sarcasm. 'I want to hear that dreadful woman's reason for being here. She owes it to Anna.'

When Anna stood up to address Heather, she looked as if she was about to explode.

'All these years have gone by during which time nothing has been heard from you,' she shouted. 'John told me about his marriage to you, and that it turned out to be a complete disaster. He also said that he was going to change his will so I let the matter drop. I would also like to know why you found it necessary to hide during his funeral?' A look of surprise crossed Heather's face, and Anna continued her tirade. 'Yes, you were seen hiding behind a tree. Don't you think that the polite thing would have been to let us know you were coming?'

The expression on Heather's face didn't change. 'I didn't want to be seen by anyone at the funeral. I wanted to say my goodbyes to John in private. I also knew the kind of reception I would receive from all of you, and I was right of course. People don't change. I'm sorry if my sudden appearance caused you any grief. When I married John all those years ago, not one member of this family was happy about it. You all made it quite plain that I wasn't good enough for him, and that is just one of the reasons why we separated. You managed to ruin our future together. But having said that, and despite everything, I… I have always loved John, and I always will.'

'And now, I can only assume that you are expecting

some enormous financial gain, after all these years of utter silence,' Anna retorted.

Heather was obviously stung by this barbed comment, and her voice wavered as she continued. 'There's… there is something that you, and the family might not know. We had a son, but as there was so much bitterness between us, I guess that John didn't tell any of you about him.'

'A son, but…' Anna looked stunned, and the rest of the people in the room looked at one another in surprise.

'Please let me go on,' Heather continued. 'Of course I knew that John hadn't written another will. As we were still married, Mr. Parker naturally kept me in the picture.' The solicitor looked uncomfortable when Anna turned to look at him.

'So I was right. You are only here for the money,' Anna said bitterly.

'Unfortunately, our son… John Joseph has a severe neurological condition, which means that he has to receive constant medical attention. I feel that it is only fair that some of his father's estate should go towards his long-term care, especially if anything ever happens to me. So, if it can be arranged, I intend to accept a small portion of the estate to help with this. Hopefully this money can be put in trust for my son until such time as he needs it.' Heather put out her hands and looked at everyone in the room. 'The rest… is all yours, and I hope it makes you all very happy. You won't be hearing from me again, so goodbye.'

Heather Armitage walked up to the desk, shook hands with Mr. Parker and, with her head held high, she left the room.

There was a stunned silence, as everyone digested what she'd said.

Molly felt sorry for Heather. The poor woman was obviously not interested in receiving all the money from

John's estate, but her love for her son had brought her all the way across the Atlantic to get enough financial help for their son's long-term care. Had this hostile family no love, or even sorrow for this child?

Molly looked at everyone, including Adam. Their faces seemed to be filled with hatred and suspicion. She felt totally confused, and shook her head slowly. She'd been on the verge of falling in love with him, but now she felt as if she didn't know him at all. He'd been angry and cold towards her during the committal ceremony, but she'd assumed that he was mourning the loss of his cousin. Are his true colours beginning to show, she asked herself? She shifted in her seat and sighed heavily, but Adam didn't seem to notice.

Could she in all honesty tie herself to a family like that, she wondered. Her answer had to be 'No'.

Without thinking any further, she stood up, and without looking back, walked out of the room, closing the door firmly behind her; she wasn't only closing the door on her relationship with Adam, but to the sound of the bitter recriminations, and selfishness that were emanating from that crowded room. Molly didn't wish to be a part of this family now, or at any other time in the future.

'Goodbye Adam,' she whispered as she left the building.

AUBURN LIES

Why should she sit around this place feeling sorry for herself all the time? George wasn't worth all this angst and misery, Janet Henderson told herself as she looked into the mirror on her dressing table. 'Oh my God, do I look dreadful, or do I look dreadful?'

Her 42nd birthday was looming and her puffy, red-rimmed eyes stared back at her mournfully. She noted that even her laughter lines had somehow become deep trenches. Her over-long brown hair was out of shape, and rapidly reverting to its true colour... a kind of streaky grey. This is what George Henderson had done to her, and the time had come to put away all thoughts of her worthless husband. No, she thought: from now on, she was going to call him her ex-husband.

Janet stood up and walked miserably out into the kitchen, She shivered as she looked at the view from the window of her apartment. It was a cold February morning, and everything seemed to be covered by a glistening layer of frost. But at least the sky was a beautiful blue this morning, she said with a smile as she sat down to eat her breakfast. Janet had always been a happy and cheerful person until George had walked out of her life. She stood up, grabbed hold of both ends of the tie on her old quilted dressing gown, and tied them together firmly around her thickening waist.

'Oh, he's welcome to that... that Beaumont woman. I wonder how she copes with George's bad temper first thing in the morning.' She couldn't help laughing. 'I really should have told her that he snores loudly every night.'

Janet smiled as she imagined the beautiful, young Poppie Beaumont clamping her smooth, unlined hands over her ears, whilst desperately trying to get to sleep.

'She is so welcome to him,' she said placing her feet into the cosy warmth of her slippers, and wandering out of the kitchen. George had walked away from their marriage six whole weeks ago, and she was at last coming to terms with the fact that he wasn't coming back. Her nights were sublimely silent, and she was able to eat her breakfast in peace each morning. She could even choose whichever cereal she wanted, and could eat two slices of toast instead of the statutory one slice that George always insisted upon.

Janet giggled. She could even go back to bed and read a chick lit novel. Oh how scornful he used to be, if she even as much as looked at such a book in the local book shop. It was definitely not the sort of genre that he thought his wife should be reading.

She lifted up her hair, and turned her head both ways trying to get a better look at it. 'I think I'll have my hair cut,' she said, smiling to herself when she remembered how much George hated short hair. 'I think I'll have it tinted again, but not the usual boring brown colour. Perhaps I could have some blond streaks this time?'

Janet's forehead creased with consternation. No, that wouldn't do at all. Poppie Beaumont had some nasty blond streaks in her hair, and she didn't wish to look like her. Perhaps she could try an auburn tint this time: she could be a fiery and sexy redhead. She placed her hands on her hips and paraded around the room. For the first time since George had left her, she felt free. She no longer cared what he thought anymore, or what he did.

She heard the letter box clang. She walked out into the hall, picked up the local newspaper, and sat down at the kitchen table to read it. There was nothing much of interest to her, until her eyes locked on to an item in the advertisement section under **DATING AGENCIES**.

Dating Agencies, she thought. Could she? No, not that one... but this one might do mightn't it? It could be me, couldn't it? Janet turned back to the advert to read it again. Without stopping to think any further, or be the cautious person she usually was, she picked up her mobile phone and tapped in the agency's number.

'Good morning, The Sure Shot Dating Agency here, can I help you?'

'Yes, good morning. I'd like to enrol with your agency please,' Janet said trying to make her voice sound a little younger.

'Well then madam, perhaps you could tell me something about yourself for our records?' The woman sounded a little obsequious as she continued, 'We will of course send you a form so that we can put all your details into our computer. But first, we would like a general picture. Could you describe yourself for me, please?'

'Yes of course. My... my name is... Antonia... Antonia Denton, and I've been working as a model. I'm... 29,' Janet said with her fingers well and truly crossed. 'Unmarried of course, slim and some people say, quite pretty. My hair is... auburn and my eyes are a rather nice shade of blue. Oh yes, I'm a Cancerian and I'm looking for a man with...'

To Janet's surprise, only two days later, a letter arrived from the agency. She stared at it for a while before opening the envelope. Doubt began to sweep over her in waves when her hand, and the letter, hovered over the waste bin. It took her several minutes more before she could pluck up enough courage to tear the envelope open. Her hands shook as she withdrew the form it contained, and as she read the first paragraph her resolve almost dropped to zero.

They wanted to know so much about her. There were so many personal questions about her, her life and her appearance, so how could she be honest after what she'd said on the phone?

A sudden picture of Poppie Beaumont imprinted itself into her mind, and her latent sense of fun, which had almost been extinguished by George, encouraged her to fill it in. When she'd finished, she read it through carefully. 'Who is this person? I don't think it's me, but what the...' Janet laughed with delight. 'I wonder what kind of man the computer will find for me. It might be fun finding out, of course.' She placed the form inside the addressed envelope provided by the agency, and sealed it.

'If only George could see me now,' she said, laughing again devilishly.

Later that week, Jan left the office early, and had just returned home from an exhausting shopping session. She felt tired, and put the kettle on to make a much needed cup of tea, when her mobile buzzed insistently at her.

'Hello,' she said a little breathlessly.

'Ms. Antonia Denton?'

'Yes... yes, hello.' Her eyebrows lifted, her mouth opened... and her heart beat quickened.

'It's Nicola Hampton, from the Sure Shot Dating Agency here. Our computer has come up with what we feel is the perfect match for you.'

'You have?' Janet felt excited and terrified all at the same time.

'We were wondering if you would like to meet him.'

Janet's knees began to shake. What was she doing? But nothing daunted she ignored her worries, and found herself saying, 'Why yes I... I would. Where and when?'

'Would tomorrow night be convenient for you, under the large clock in London's Waterloo Station? I know it's a very popular meeting place, but it has worked well for our clients over the years.'

'Yes... yes of c... course,' Janet stuttered. 'I've never done this kind of thing before, so how... how will I know him?'

'Some dating agencies distribute photographs of their clients, but we have a policy here not to do so,' Nicola Hampton gave a little laugh. 'We think that it adds a little mystery to the occasion, so we always suggest that each party should wear a red carnation. That usually works. Can I tell him that you'll be there at 7.00 p.m. tomorrow evening then, Antonia?'

'Yes. What's his name by the way?'

'It's Michael Parry. Perhaps you'd be good enough to let us know how the evening goes.'

'Yes, of course I will. Thank you, goodbye.' Janet switched off her mobile. What had she done? Her heart was thumping as panic began to set in. She couldn't possibly go.

'Why not?' enquired a little voice in her head.

'Because I'm...'

'A coward?' the voice intoned.

Janet stood under the clock in Waterloo Station, nervously patting her auburn tinted hair. She was waiting for a complete stranger, which was something she would never have thought of doing in the past. About four other people were also standing under the famous clock. Did they know the person they were waiting for, or were they feeling nervous and apprehensive, just like her? She felt guilty when she remembered how she'd described herself, because the only thing on that form which was true, was the colour of her hair; the rest was pure fiction.

It was just after 7.00 p.m., and she was beginning to feel cold and rather silly. When she'd left her office, she'd felt quite confident, but now all she wanted to do was to go home. What on earth had made her do it? It was completely out of character. She looked up at the clock again. Michael Parry was late, and probably has had second thoughts about the whole thing, which was just as well, she concluded.

Janet had spent the afternoon at the hairdressers and she patted her hair again. She wasn't quite sure if she liked the colour, and it was very short. She looked up at the clock yet again. 'He's definitely not coming,' she said, 'and I can't say that I blame him. I think he'll be very disappointed if he does come. He'll be hoping to meet a beautiful 29 year-old with a model's figure, and here am I, a dumpy, frumpy woman of near middle age, wearing the most uncomfortably high-heeled shoes imaginable. I'm definitely wasting my time... and his.'

Janet fingered the carnation sitting a little limply in the lapel of her new pale green suit, and looked around with anxiety spreading over her in waves. 'I shouldn't have lied about my appearance,' she whispered. 'How on earth did I allow myself to get into such a ridiculous situation?'

Suddenly she felt a light tap on her shoulder.

'Hello. Are you Antonia? I'm so sorry I'm late, but the train was delayed.'

Janet turned round. A rather handsome man stared down at her. He had a beard and was wearing a black trench coat with the collar turned up. He also sported a red carnation.

'Yes, that's me and you must be Michael Par...?'

Loud alarm bells began to clamour in Janet's mind, and the words froze on her lips, as she looked deeply into his eyes.

Recognition flared, and her heart lurched.

'George...?'

'Janet... ?'

GOING TO THE ZOO

'Come on Dad, let's go, pleeease,' eleven year old Jamie said as he tugged at his father's sleeve. 'I'm so bored. We've seen this so many times.' He kicked a small stone near his foot, and it rolled quickly to the other side of the path. 'Dad, can we go now?' He closed his eyes in frustration.

They were staring at a large male gorilla sitting in the centre of its cage, and it stared back at them with its small intelligent eyes. Jamie was just wondering what a gorilla would, or could be thinking about, when the animal pulled a face, and turned its back on them. He was obviously bored too, and fed up with seeing us, Jamie thought as they moved along to the next cage.

'I wish we could do something else for a change, Dad,' he suddenly blurted out. 'Could we go to a football match? My teacher said that I'm getting quite good at football.' He felt slightly guilty, because he loved his father, and didn't want to appear ungrateful. 'One of my friends at school was telling me about this place that's ginormous and full of trampolines. It sounds super fun. Could we go there?' Even though Jamie knew how difficult life was for his Dad, deep down he knew that he had to say something. He's only responsible for me one day each week, he thought, and we're running out of places to visit. Jamie yawned.

His father looked down at him, with a worried look on his face. 'Yes son. We could do something different next week, if that's what you want. I'll look into it for you.' They sauntered along a well-known pathway, and Jamie yawned again. He'd been thinking about his favourite game on his iPhone. His friend Andrew had said that he'd be playing the game that day, and would probably boast that his score would be much larger than his.

Jamie looked up at the sky, and his shoulders slumped. Huge black clouds were hovering overhead, and he felt the first heavy drops of rain. He was finding it difficult to pretend that he was enjoying himself, but in this horrid weather even the animals were looking miserable.

'Race you to the tea room,' his father called out.

'I bet I'll win, Dad,' Jamie shouted as he tried to overtake him.

They reached the little café wet and out of breath. Jamie managed to find somewhere for them to sit, and his Dad queued up to buy them some lunch. Jamie was hoping that he didn't buy the usual cheese and tomato sandwiches, as he didn't really like them. He knew his Dad was doing his best, but he was looking miserable too, as he stared at the dozen or so hungry customers standing in front of him.

Jamie thought that now would be a good time to talk to him about coming back home to live with them. They'd been apart for months now, and neither of them was happy. He looked at his father. His sense of fun had almost disappeared, and his mouth turned down at the edges most of the time. Why didn't his mum and dad get on now? They used to be so happy. Jamie knew that his father felt that the time they spent together was precious, and that they should be enjoying themselves. But he could see the tears in his father's eyes as he placed a steaming hot, but weak cup of tea in front of Jamie. 'At least the tea's hot, son,' he said as he slumped down on the uncomfortable wooden chair. 'I'm sorry but we have to have cheese and tomato, because they've run out of all the other fillings.'

'Yes Dad,' Jamie mumbled. He tried to think of something cheerful to say, but he was feeling cold and wet, and nothing he could think of seemed right. His hair dripped down his face and he brushed it away in frustration.

His Dad looked at him and smiled. 'Whilst I was

69

waiting in the queue, I was thinking about where we could go next Sunday. I was planning to go to the beach again, but if you'd rather go to this trampoline place, we could look it up on the internet for details,' he said ruffling his young son's blond curly hair.

'Could you, Dad? That would be ace. Perhaps my friend Andrew could come with us.'

'Yes, that would make a really good change. I should have thought about doing something else a long time ago.' But once again, his eyes drooped downwards, and he seemed to shrink back into his chair.

Now's my chance, Jamie thought. He steeled himself to ask his father the question which had been burning inside him for ages. He had to say something.

'Dad?'

'Yes, Jamie?'

'You do still love Mum and me, don't you?' His father looked startled. 'You can't really enjoy living in that little flat on your own, when we've so much room back at the house.'

'Of course I still love you Jamie.'

'Well, what's stopping you from coming back home to live with us again then?'

'Jamie, it's not as simple as that. Your mother and I…' His father stopped speaking, and put his head in his hands. When he looked up again, he said, 'When you're older you'll understand, you'll see.'

'But Dad, I'll be twelve soon. I'm not a baby,' he replied, sitting up in his seat and trying to look grown up. He felt disgruntled. Why do adults always say things like that? 'I need to know now, Dad. Why won't you discuss it with me?'

'You wouldn't understand,' his father said.

After they'd finished their lunch, they left the little café, and as it had stopped raining, they continued to look at all the birds and animals. Jamie hated the fact that they were all living in cages and not free to enjoy their lives naturally. He tried to imagine what it would be like, but failed miserably. Once it started raining again they raced back to the car.

Later, his father dropped him off at home, and was just about to drive away, when his mother invited him in for a cup of tea. He stayed for several hours, and even had a meal with them. Afterwards, Jamie tried hard not to listen to their discussions, and decided to go up to his room. But the sound of their hushed, and sometimes angry voices drifted upstairs, and he felt that he couldn't bear to listen anymore. He pulled his duvet up over his ears, and eventually cried himself to sleep.

His mother's voice woke him the following morning, as she called upstairs. 'Jamie please get up now. I won't be able to give you a lift to school if you don't hurry. I must get to work on time today.' A few minutes later, he heard the sudden noise of breaking crockery and his mother's brief, but telling swearword. Her voice sounded hurt and angry, and he put his head underneath the duvet; he had the beginnings of a stomach ache.

A few minutes later his mother came into his room carrying a cup of tea on a tray. 'Jamie, why aren't you up yet? Come on.' He looked at her over the edge of his red and white striped duvet. She was still a really pretty woman he thought, despite her age. After all she was nearly thirty-five, and two years younger than Dad. Her hair was blond and curly just like his. Her eyes used to be bright, and her smile always made him feel good, but this morning her face looked puffy, as if she'd been crying. Nothing had changed: his father had gone, and he felt really disappointed.

Jamie suddenly felt his mother's hand on his forehead.

'Are you feeling alright, Jamie?' she asked, anxiety creeping into her voice. 'I've made you a cup of tea. Please drink it, and then you must get up.'

'No Mum,' he said desperately trying to make his voice sound weak. 'I've got a tummy ache. Do I have to go to school today?'

'Jamie you don't feel as if you have a temperature darling, but if you're really not feeling well perhaps you shouldn't go to school today. I have to go to work now, but I'll be back at about twelve o'clock. You will be alright on your own won't you?'

'Yes Mum, of course I will. I don't need a baby-sitter,' he said as he snuggled back down under the comfort and warmth of his bed.

'Well, use the phone if you need me, please Jamie.' She leant over, kissed him on the forehead and left the room with a worried expression on her face. A few minutes later, he heard her leave the house. He stayed in his bed for a while feeling utterly miserable. His Sunday excursions with his father were becoming more and more difficult. When he was younger and his parents had been happy, they'd enjoyed going out for the day together, but now... Jamie knew he had to think of some way to bring his parents back together again. He closed his eyes tightly.

The solution came to him in a flash.

He could disappear for a couple of days, and he knew exactly where he would go. That way his parents would have to get together in order to look for him. Jamie got up, washed quickly and ate a bowl of cereal. Afterwards, he felt excited, and the ache in his stomach lessened. He took some bottled water and food out of the fridge. After making himself a few rounds of sandwiches, he placed them in a box, before taking it all upstairs to his bedroom. His suitcase was on top of his wardrobe, so he had to stand on a chair to get it down, and he placed it on his bed. He quickly put everything he needed in the case, made his bed and tidied his room slightly. Jamie felt slightly apprehensive as he looked around his room, before walking downstairs and leaving the house.

Jamie and a few of his friends often played in an old derelict house, despite being warned that it was unsafe. They told themselves that it was haunted and played 'ghost' games in the large and echoing rooms. They discovered an old mattress and some rickety furniture in a ramshackle garden shed, and made one of the rooms habitable. They described it to some envious girls at school, as being "their pad". It took about fifteen minutes to walk to the house. He was surprised and disappointed to find that it now had a fence around it and all the doors and windows were boarded up too.

A notice in the front garden read: "**PLEASE KEEP OUT – DANGEROUS STRUCTURE**". Ignoring his mother's warning to stay away from this old house, Jamie managed to climb through a hole in the fence, and he made his way round to the back garden to see if he could find a way in. He soon discovered that one of the windows was broken. It was wide open, and made a horrible squeaking noise as it swung from side to side in the strengthening breeze. The boards which had been covering it were lying splintered and scattered on the ground. Jamie was quite tall for his age, and he climbed inside without much difficulty.

Because of the shutters, it was eerily dark inside the old house, and Jamie felt a little scared, but his determination grew as he found his way to their pad. When he opened the door, it seemed really creepy. He heard a strange noise which made him jump, and he stood still for a while until his eyes adjusted to the dark, but because he was on his own, his resolve began to waver. The room was cold and he started to shiver. Then he remembered why he was here. 'Don't be silly,' Jamie told himself. 'There's no reason to be scared.'

As he walked towards the window, there was a loud crack, and without any warning, the floor beneath his feet gave way. Jamie cried out when he felt himself falling, but there was nobody around to hear him…

The room was situated over a large, damp cellar, and he fell awkwardly onto a pile of old sacking, some of which was spread over the cold stone floor. He felt a moment's panic as pain shot throughout his body, and… everything went blank.

Jamie's mother, Amanda, came home about an hour later, because she'd been worried about leaving him at home on his own. The house seemed unusually quiet as she walked through the front door.

'Jamie, it's me. Are you O.K?' she called out. There was no answer, so she hurried upstairs. She knew something was wrong as soon as she walked into his room. It was empty and quite tidy for the first time in ages. Her heart began to pound alarmingly, when she noticed that his suitcase was missing, and after opening a drawer, she realised that some of his clothes had gone too. She raced into the bathroom, only to find that his wash bag was missing.

Amanda began to panic. 'Where on earth is he? Where would he have gone on his own?' Her forehead creased with worry. Perhaps he'd gone to Robert's flat, she thought as she raced downstairs and dialled her husband's office number.

'Hello, Robert Watson speaking. How can I help you?' Amanda thought his voice sounded confident, and quite unlike the way he'd spoken to her yesterday.

'Robert, it's me, Amanda.'

74

'Yes, what do you want? Although I wouldn't think that we had much left to say to one another, after last night,' he added his tone cold, and to the point.

'It's not about last night. I'm worried about Jamie.'

'What… what do you mean, Amanda? He's not… he's not ill, is he? Please tell me that he's alright. I couldn't bear it if he was upset because of me,' he said showing instant concern.

Amanda explained what had happened, and the fact that he was now missing. 'I thought he might have gone to your flat,' she said in desperation.

'Why the hell did you leave him on his own? He's only eleven years old! I'd have thought…'

'You know perfectly well that since you left us, I have to work. My God, you're a callous…'

'Of all the stupid…' Robert stopped in mid-sentence, and Amanda heard him take a deep breath. 'Look, this isn't getting us anywhere.' The tone of his voice altered. It became softer, but with a growing sense of urgency. 'We have to think rationally. Where would he have gone?' He was silent for a few seconds. 'Look Amanda, meet me at my flat in twenty minutes. I'm leaving the office now.'

'Do you think we ought to inform the police?'

'No, I don't think so. We must try to find him ourselves first, O.K?'

'Yes, yes of course. Oh Robert, you do think he'll be alright, don't you?'

'I'm sure he will, after all, he's a sensible lad.'

'I hope you're right.'

When they both arrived at the flat, they found that Jamie wasn't there. They looked at one another, and Amanda began to cry. Her shoulders heaved with pent up emotion, and Robert put his arms gently around her shoulders. 'Amanda please don't cry. We have to think logically,' he said waving his hands about. 'Does he have a favourite place, or somewhere he goes to play with friends perhaps?'

'Well, there's that old house at the bottom of Rectory Road, but I'm sure he wouldn't have gone there. I don't think it's all that safe. They've erected a tall wire fence around the site, and I saw a man boarding up some of the windows the other day, too.' She took a deep breath. 'I'd already told Jamie not to go near it again. But I honestly can't remember if I told him that it was boarded up.'

'Come on. I bet that's where he is.'

As they drove up to the old house, Amanda noticed that a large sign had been erected in front of the wire fence. They climbed out of the car and raced over to read it. 'Robert, the small print on this Council notice says that it is a dangerous structure, and it's going to be demolished next week. Surely Jamie can't be in there, as it's all boarded up, and I'm certain he couldn't have got through the fence either.'

Robert's face turned white with worry, and beads of perspiration appeared on his forehead as he looked along the fence. 'Amanda, look, there's already a hole in the fence over there? I'll see if I can get through it. Wait here and I'll take a look.'

'Do hurry. I've got an awful feeling about this,' Amanda said anxiously, as she paced up and down.

A few minutes later, Robert rushed back to her side. 'I managed to get through the hole in the fence and there's an open window round the back. It seems very dark in there because of the shuttering on all the windows, so can you get me the torch from the glove compartment? I think I can just about squeeze in through the window.'

'Robert, please be careful,' she said.

It seemed an age whilst he was in the house, during which time Amanda's fears for their safety increased.

A sudden shout made her jump. 'Amanda, I've found Jamie lying on the cellar floor. I think the floor must have given way. This place is a death-trap!'

'Is he... is he alright, Robert?' Her heart began to thump wildly.

'I don't know. He's unconscious. We have to call for an ambulance. Have you got your mobile?'

'Yes. I'll do it right away. Oh my God. I don't believe this,' she said as she found her mobile in her handbag, and with fumbling fingers, tapped in 999. Several minutes later a paramedic team arrived, and they smashed their way through the fence. After breaking the lock on the front door of the old house, they were able to get inside. How Amanda managed to keep sane, she will never know, as it seemed an age before the men came out again carrying Jamie on a stretcher. He looked pale, and his eyes were closed. She began to panic when she saw a huge livid bruise on the side of his face, and one on his temple. 'Oh Jamie, why did you go in there?'

Amanda and Robert both stood helplessly looking down at him. Jamie moaned slightly as he was placed in the ambulance, and once the doors had been closed securely, a member of the team handed them a small suitcase.

'I assume this belongs to your son? It was lying beside him.'

'Yes, it's Jamie's,' Amanda whispered.

The young paramedics climbed quickly into the ambulance and drove away.

The fact that the siren was screaming sent waves of panic and regret coursing throughout her whole body.

'Robert, he was running away from our hurtful words last night. Oh, I should never have left him, but I'm worried about my job, and I had no alternative. Thank goodness I came home early.' More tears streamed down her stricken face. 'Oh Jamie, what have we done to you?'

'We must go to the hospital now.' Robert looked frightened and grim as they climbed into his car, and they sped off in the direction of the local Hospital.

Once Jamie was examined, he was taken up to the Intensive Care Unit. He was still unconscious, and Robert and Amanda sat by his bedside. Amanda didn't say very much, because she imagined that just like her, Robert was feeling guilty. But, it was neither the time, nor the place for reprisals or recriminations, as their thoughts were centred on Jamie's condition, and whether he would recover.

When the doctor on duty came into the room, they looked up at him expectantly.

'Good afternoon, Mr. and Mrs. Watson,' he said. 'I'm Peter Howard. As you can see, Jamie is still unconscious. He's suffering from concussion, and has fractured one of the bones in his right arm. The other injuries are generally superficial, thank goodness.'

'But will he be...' Amanda found it difficult to talk. 'Will... will he be alright?'

'Well, Jamie has had a nasty fall, and we are keeping him under careful observation. Head injuries can be difficult to assess, and we are hopeful that he will soon gain consciousness, and we will then know a little more. I'm sorry I can't be any more forthcoming.'

Robert stood up and walked anxiously around the room. 'Thank you doctor, we appreciate your candour. We can sit with him for a while?'

'Yes, of course. Well I must continue on my rounds. I'll call in a little later to see how he is.'

Amanda looked down at her son, and tears began to stream down her face 'Robert' she said, 'What if...'

'Amanda, please don't...' he said. 'I feel as guilty about

it as you do.' He walked over to her side… and put his arms around her.

She looked up at him. 'I keep thinking about what we said to one another last night. I'm so sorry and I didn't mean what I said. Life has been so difficult without you.'

'Yes, I know it has,' he said. 'What on earth were we thinking about? How can we forgive ourselves if he doesn't recover?' Amanda shook her head, and sat down on a chair beside her son's bed, and Robert sat miserably beside her. 'Amanda, Jamie has been feeling really upset about us being apart, and he asked me if we could get back together again.' They linked hands sadly, as they looked down at their son.

Jamie stirred. He felt strange, and his head ached. Where was he, because the last thing he remembered was being in the old house? He tried to move, but everything else ached as well. When he tried to open his eyes intense pain took over, and everything went black.

About two hours later, he woke up again, and this time he felt a little better. He managed to open his eyes, and the first thing he saw was a scene that sent his spirits soaring. His mother and father were sitting next to one another, and for once they were not arguing. In fact, they were smiling down at him and, more to the point, they were holding hands!

'Hello Mum. Hello Dad,' he said quietly, with a smile on his battered face.

'Oh Jamie darling, thank goodness you're alright,' his mother said, smiling through her tears. 'How are you feeling, because you had a really bad fall? I can't imagine what you were doing in that old house? I told you never to go near it again didn't I?'

'Yes, Mum, you did, but…'

'Your Dad and I have been so worried about you, darling. You've been unconscious for some time as you knocked your head badly when you fell, and you've broken one of the bones in your arm. You will have to stay here for a few days until you feel better.'

'And will you both be visiting me together? I really need both of you here.' His parents looked at one another and smiled. 'And does this mean that you'll be coming back home to live with us again, Dad?' he said, his voice cracking with emotion. 'Please say you will.'

'Well Jamie, your mother and I have a lot of thinking and talking to do. All this has made us both realise just how much we love you… and each other.' He turned to Amanda. 'I would love to come home; that's if you'll have me back,' he said putting his arm tenderly around Amanda's shoulders. 'My flat isn't very comfortable.'

She smiled through her tears. 'Yes Robert, I would love you to come back home. I think it is high time that we sorted everything out. We can't go on like this, can we?'

'No, we can't,' Robert said squeezing her hand. He turned round to talk to Jamie. 'Now then young man, I want you to promise us that you will never ever do such a silly thing again.'

'I promise I won't Dad.' Jamie felt weak and a little woozy, but happy for the first time in months… his parents were together again at last. 'Do you know something,' he said lying back against his pillow, 'I know that I shouldn't have run away, but I had a feeling that my plan would work.'

'Your plan?' His parents said in unison.

'Yes, a plan. I had to have one. I wanted you to come back home again, Dad. We weren't very happy without you.'

Robert took hold of his son's hand gently. 'Your plan certainly worked, and I wish with all my heart that it hadn't been necessary. Going into that old house wasn't a very intelligent thing to do, was it?'

'No Dad, it wasn't, and I promise you that I'll never do anything like that again, and...' He hesitated.

'And?' his mother said softly.

'I'm really sorry for scaring you both, but you see I... I was so fed up with visiting the ZOO!'

A DOLL FOR CHRISTMAS

Five year old Chloe felt so excited. She was standing at the bus stop with her mother, and staring at her favourite toy shop window to see if the little doll that she loved was still there. It was. In fact the little doll seemed to be smiling at her.

'Mummy… Mummy?' Chloe said, tugging at her sleeve.

'Yes darling?'

'Mummy, do you think my letter reached Father Christmas in time?' It was the day before Christmas Eve and they were waiting for the bus, which was already a little late.

'I'm sure it did, darling,' her mother said. 'Where is that bus?' But Chloe was bored, and she kicked a stone and sent it spinning into the gutter. 'Don't do that, Chloe please?' she pleaded. 'You'll wear your shoes out, and I can't afford to buy you any new ones before Christmas – or at any other time either,' she added sadly under her breath. She looked up at the sky. It was only 4 o'clock in the afternoon, and it was much darker than usual, even for this time of the year. The clouds looked menacing. She shivered, and pulled her collar up around her neck.

'Can I go and look at the stop window then, Mummy? Pleeease?'

'Yes, but be quick as the bus will be here soon, and we don't want to miss it, do we? I don't like the look of this weather.'

Chloe raced over to the shop, and stared hard at the toy shop window. It was lit up just like a Christmas tree. She pressed her nose up against the pane of glass. It felt really cold, but she could see the thing she wanted more than anything in the whole wide world, much more clearly that way. The little doll sat on a box looking at her with just a hint of a smile on her face. 'If only I could have you for Christmas,' she whispered, 'cos you're so pretty.'

'Mummy?' she called out suddenly.

'Yes Chloe?'

'Do you 'member…?'

'Chloe do come and stand here next to me. The bus will be along any minute now. I think it will either rain or turn to sleet soon,' she said, moving her feet from side to side.

'Mummy, I would like… do you think I could have that little dolly in the window, please? Don't you 'member, it's the one I showed you the other day?' Her mother walked over and stood beside her. 'Look, it's that one over there with the pink dress and the happy face. She's got lovely blond hair just like mine. She's got black shiny shoes too.'

'Darling, I would love you to have her, but as I said, I can't afford it this year,' her mother replied, quickly returning to the bus stop.

'But Mummy,' Chloe wailed, rubbing the tears from her eyes. 'My friend Claire's mummy has bought her a dolly, so can I have one? Please?' She couldn't take her eyes off the doll's face. 'Oohh… I wish… I wish… I wish…' she said, concentrating hard and screwing up her pretty blue eyes.

She put her head on one side to see if she could see how much it was. A little white tag was attached to the doll's hand. Yes, she could just see some squiggles on it. There was a sort of an 'L' with a little line through it. That was a pound sign she thought proudly. Next to it was a figure '1' – she recognised it 'cos it was the first number she had ever learned at her nursery school. Next to the '1' was a '0' and Chloe was quite sure that a '0' was a nothing.' Oh goody,' she said, 'the doll doesn't cost much at all,' she said excitedly.

Chloe knew that her mother wanted her to stay with her at the bus stop, but she couldn't tear herself away from the shop window. She was mesmerised by all the tinsel and the coloured flashing lights. There were teddy bears with black noses, appealing faces and bright buttony eyes. There was a doll's house with pretty red curtains, and a real light inside. Some toy soldiers stood to attention in front of a toy fort. 'They're all painted red, just like the post box outside our house.' A pile of bricks had large letters painted on them. 'There's an 'A',' she said concentrating hard, 'and… and there's a 'B' and a 'C',' she added, feeling really pleased with herself.

A clown with a funny face seemed to stare at her. She didn't like his eyes much, and she looked away. Suddenly a toy train came into view, and rattled past her nose making her jump, before it disappeared into a small tunnel and out of sight.

Despite all the colourful toys in the window, Chloe's eyes kept going back to the little doll. By now she was quite sure she was smiling at her, and not only that, she was even holding out her arms to her. *She'll have such a sad Christmas if nobody buys her, 'coz she'll be sitting all alone in this cold shop window*, Chloe thought miserably. *P'raps when my daddy comes home, he will buy her for me. I haven't seen him since he went into that hospital place, and Mummy is so unhappy all the time.*

Everything now hinged on whether Father Christmas had received her letter. Chloe remembered seeing him in the big shop in town last week. She closed her eyes tightly, so that she could picture him reading it. His clothes and hood were all red and edged with white fur. His black shiny boots, the black buttons on his coat, together with his long white flowing beard, made him look very old indeed. His big round eyes sparkled and flashed, as he threw back his head, saying, 'Ho, ho, ho.'

'Oh, how I wish… I wish… I wish.'

A snowflake fell on Chloe's nose, and was immediately followed by another, and… the picture faded. 'Ooohh look… it's snowing Mummy, just in time for Christmas. We'll be able to make a snowman,' she called out in delight. Chloe turned back to look at the window again, but her breath, and the cold weather, had made the thickened glass mist over. To her utmost dismay, she lost sight of everything in the shop window.

'Do come away from that window, Chloe,' her mother called out to her.

'No,' Chloe answered her stubbornly. 'I don't want to leave her. Her name is Katy. I'm going to call her Katy.'

'Come on Chloe, please?' Her mother was growing impatient. 'I won't tell you again.'

'Katy will be so unhappy Mummy,' she said sadly. 'She'll be cold in the snow.'

'Chloe, I'm getting a little tired of this. Please come over here.'

Chloe took a last loving look at the window, and walked back to her mother's side. 'If I can't have her today, can I come back tomorrow, please? I really do want her.'

Her mother's tone softened. 'Look darling, I would love you to have the dolly, but I don't have enough money with me to buy her for you.'

'Well p'raps Daddy will buy it then.'

'Chloe, my darling,' tears began to fill her mother's eyes, 'how can I get you to understand that Daddy is never coming home again?'

'But Mummy, he must come home.' Hot, prickly tears began to well up in Chloe's eyes too. She looked up at her mother. 'P'raps Father Christmas will bring me a doll just like Katy? Oh I wish… I wish… I wish.'

An elderly man with white flowing hair and a fur hat

now stood at the bus stop. He'd been listening intently to their conversation.

'Good evening, madam,' he said smiling and gently tilting his hat. 'Perhaps you would allow me to be your daughter's Father Christmas this year? It would give me the greatest pleasure.' He quickly pressed a £10 note into Chloe's mother's hand. 'Please say you will accept it? My children are all grown up now, you see. A Happy Christmas to you both.'

'Thank you, and a happy Christmas to you too... but I don't think that I can accept this.' She looked down at the note in her hand for a few moments. 'It's really very kind of you,' she finally managed to blurt out. 'But I can't let you do this.' She turned round to speak to him, but he'd gone!

The street was completely deserted.

Chloe was overjoyed; her wish had been granted. 'Ooohh Mummy, that man says he was my Father Christmas! Can I have that dolly now, and was he really Father Christmas?,' she said finally taking a breath.

'I... I don't know, darling,' she replied gently. 'Perhaps he was.'

'He really did get my letter then,' Chloe said happily rushing over to the window again just to make sure that the Katy doll was still there, and to her delight, she was. Chloe could just see her through the misty shop window. She stared hard at her, and to her surprise, saw what she thought were tears streaming down the doll's cheeks.

'Yes, it certainly looks like it,' her mother replied with a smile. Chloe started to cry, only not with sadness, but with happiness. Her mother looked down at her, and brushed away her tears saying, 'Come on darling, let's go in and buy the little Katy doll before the bus comes, shall we?'

PORTRAIT OF A DREAM

I couldn't believe it, my dream man was back after all this time. My heart pounded with excitement and wonder. He was standing on the other side of the courtyard staring at me. I was totally lost and under his spell again.

'Come to me, please come to me,' he murmured. His voice was as soft as velvet, and despite the distance between us, it floated towards me as if on a zephyr breeze. His long robe had golden edges that gleamed like the early morning sunshine, and his long blond hair moved gently as he moved his head. He was magnificent. A cry of pleasure escaped from my lips as his outstretched arms beckoned to me. 'Come to me my dearest. It is time and I need you... oh how I need you,' he pleaded.

Recognition flared briefly in my brain, as his deep blue eyes bored into mine, piercing my soul and heightening my already receptive senses. Pure joy, strange distantly remembered love, longing and peace settled over me like a warm silken blanket. I was being cosseted; I was a compliant, happy slave: a helpless moth hovering and flitting over a flame as I ran towards him.

I could feel the sun filtering through the gently swaying palm trees circling the courtyard. A heady intoxicating perfume exuded from the tropical plants surrounding the ornate fountain in the centre, and the sound of water trickling and flowing over stones was like gentle music to my ears. This was a peaceful paradise, interrupted only by the sound of bees fluttering their sun-drenched golden wings all around me.

I was nearly there.

I woke suddenly. I was sweating profusely, and I sighed deeply. Wow, Sue! That was only a dream, and I haven't had one like that for such a long time. It was still dark outside and the digital clock on the bedside cabinet beside me, glowed clinically. It was only 5 a.m. I heard the insistent sound of a police car's siren as it sped beneath my window. I groaned. I needed to be back in that beautiful courtyard with him. Instead, all I could hear was the rainwater splashing and gurgling noisily down the drainpipe outside my window.

I sleep alone, but not by choice you understand. You see my husband Michael had decided that we were no longer compatible. His feelings for me had gone, been extinguished, or whatever else you may say about the loss of love. He moved out two days' later, the rat, and it was only last week that I finally signed the divorce papers.

Of course I still miss Michael: we'd been married for eight childless years for heaven's sake. And as usual, my eyes searched for his familiar shape beside me. But for once, the fact that he wasn't there didn't fill me with pain and anguish. Instead, I was filled with a kind of wondrous optimism. Throughout my life, my dreams had conjured up a man with deep, gentian-blue eyes and long flowing hair. Unaccountably, the dreams had stopped once I'd married Michael. Now they'd started again, only this time I'd allowed my dream man's eyes to pierce my vulnerability, and finally my soul.

But why was this happening to me?

With a languid sigh, I stretched and snuggled back under my duvet again. I wanted to be back with this beautiful man who always had such a profound effect upon my senses. If I couldn't have him in reality, then I would have to be with him in my dreams.

The next thing I knew was the sound of my mobile phone ringing, and fumbling sleepily I picked it up.

'He... Hello.'

'Hi. You took a long time to answer.' It was my best friend, Liz.

'Sorry Liz, I was fast asleep, and I'm absolutely zonked. I had a disturbed night.'

'What, another one?'

'Yes,' I replied, desperately trying not to yawn.

'Are you doing anything today?' Liz was always trying to improve the quality of my extinct social life, bless her.

'No, nothing special, but I've got some shopping to do and the garden needs weeding.'

'Really Sue,' her friend retorted. 'What happened to that fun-loving, beautiful, blond, slim girl I used to know? Michael's a bastard. He's not worth all this angst.'

'I know!'

'You know?' her friend said sounding surprised.

'Yes, and from now on I'm going to think of him as my ex-husband.' There... now I'd said it. What brought this on, I asked myself?

'Well done,' Liz continued, 'I knew you'd come to your senses one day.'

I smiled. 'Liz, do you remember me telling you about the strange dreams I used to have?'

'Yes, they involved a rather dishy man, didn't they?' Her friend chuckled throatily.

'Well, last night I dreamt about him again, and honestly Liz, it has had a profound effect upon me. Funnily enough I find that I don't give a fig about Michael any more. Isn't it great? And I have this strange feeling that something momentous is going to happen today.'

'Something momentous?'

'Yes. You don't think that I'm going mad, do you?'

'No, of course I don't, but I do think that realism has reared its head at long last, and about time too. And yes, something momentous IS going to happen today. You're coming up to London with me.'

My head suddenly 'zinged' as a pair of gentian-blue eyes swam enticingly before me again, and my heart missed a beat. 'Well, I suppose I could,' I replied.

'Good. We'll catch the 9.37 a.m. train up to London, and then we're going to make our way to the National Gallery. It's ages since we've been, and perhaps it will encourage you to start…'

'What?'

'Painting again,' she teased. 'You can't possibly let all the hard work you've done in the past go to waste. It's all beautiful, and just sitting there in your garden shed.'

'Yes, I know it is, and you're right, I should do something with them. Oh, London sounds wonderful… but Liz?'

'Yes.'

'Why today?'

'I don't know,' she said, 'a flash of inspiration perhaps. Anyway we should be at the station at 9.20. You know what the ticket queues can be like, so you haven't got long. Bye.'

'Bye,' I said into thin air. Liz could be a little bossy sometimes, but she was right: a few hours in London would be perfect.

I climbed out of bed and rushed into the bathroom. I stared at my reflection in the mirror, and was surprised to see that my eyes looked altogether brighter. In fact they positively sparkled, but why? I walked downstairs with more energy than I can ever remember, and minutes later, I managed to eat some breakfast; lots of it in fact, which was strange because ever since Michael left, I'd merely been picking at my food!

I could hardly contain my excitement as the train pulled slowly into Charing Cross station, and no matter how hard I tried, I couldn't get rid of an all-pervading feeling of urgency. Nevertheless, Liz insisted that we had a cup of coffee first, so we sat at a small table in the station forecourt. As I sat there, I became increasingly more frustrated, and ten minutes passed by slowly before Liz stood up. 'Right,' she said, draining her cup. 'Are you ready?'

'Never more so, I can't wait to see it all. Michael was never interested in art, unless it appeared in girlie magazines of course.'

'Least said, come on.' Liz walked off.

The National Gallery was wonderful as usual. The old building always exuded an unhurried aura of respectability, and each room was a delight. There were so many differing styles, colours and sizes of pictures painted by people long since dead, but whose lives lived on in the images they'd created. Time seemed meaningless as we walked from room to room. And yet, I had the strangest feeling that I was being drawn along by an invisible thread.

But where was it taking me?

The second I walked into the next gallery, I knew. A huge painting dominated the room. It was beautiful, and it glowed with vibrant colour. 'This is what I came here to see,' I told Liz in great excitement.

She looked at me askance. 'What do you mean, Sue? I thought that I arranged this visit.'

'Well, yes you did, but...'

'Wow, you're strange sometimes,' Liz said shaking her head. 'Come on let's find the restaurant. My stomach's rumbling like an approaching storm.'

My heart sank. I'd found the thing for which I'd been unconsciously seeking, and all Liz wanted to do was eat! 'Would you mind if I stayed here for a while?' I said, sitting down on a bench in front of the painting. 'I'll only be a few minutes.'

91

'OK, but don't be too long, Sue darling. There are so many wonderfully different rooms to see, and you know how you always love to comment on them all.'

I watched her as she wandered off, and I turned my attention back to the painting. It had been unsullied by the passing years, and was still clear cut and alive. I then had the strangest and oddest feeling that I'd seen it before, so I searched for the artist's name. A small sign at the side, read "Rebecca..." but I couldn't identify her surname. It was dated "1527".

Strange, long forgotten feelings for this old painting suddenly surfaced in my brain, and I felt confused. My heart missed a beat when my eyes strayed towards the intricate marble floor at the bottom of the picture. A lone white flower struggled for life in one of the cracks, which like the branches of a tree, spread randomly across its ancient surface.

By now, my heart was thumping, wildly. What was going on? I couldn't believe what was happening. I'd been searching unconsciously for a flower like this one all my life, but without success. So what does it mean to me?

"Déjà vu... déjà vu", the flower seemed to scream at me. Vague memories fluttered like butterflies in my mind and... the invisible thread pulled me again. I looked upwards...

...and I saw the man of my dreams!

He was absolutely beautiful, and his deep-blue eyes stared back at me from the canvas. He had a glorious head of golden hair like a halo. I shuddered and took an involuntary breath.

Suddenly, a deep penetrating sigh made me jump, and I turned round. A young man was now sitting beside me, his long blond hair drawn back into a ponytail. His handsome face seemed vaguely familiar to me somehow. He was broad-shouldered and even though he was sitting down, I could see that he was tall. He wore a faded blue denim jacket, jeans, brown sandals, and he too was staring at the painting.

'My dreams... ah, it has to be a miracle,' he whispered. His soft velvety voice was as mellow as the sands of time. 'Now I know why I was drawn to this place in my dreams.'

I looked at him in amazement. 'Sorry. What did you just say?' He turned to me and smiled... and my heart flipped. I was looking at two deep gentian pools into which I wanted to plunge and lose all reason.

'Yes. 'It's a miracle,' he said softly. 'I don't know how, or why, but I'm beginning to understand why I'm here... with you.'

'Understand what...?' I spluttered. Even as I said these words, strange, but long forgotten memories began to flit wildly through my brain, and just as quickly, they began to fade. I felt utterly bereft.

The young man looked at me and his eyes searched mine for some recognition. 'I understand why we've both been drawn to this picture. You see, I remember it being painted.' He looked away and a few tears began to fall down his face, which he quickly brushed away.

'But you can't possibly remember it being painted... this picture is dated 1527!' I felt so confused. What on earth was happening? Was it all a dream? No, I tried to tell myself. I'm wide awake, and here in the National Gallery.

His voice became even softer. 'Yes, I know it was. You see, I was there.'

He looked at me again, and... I couldn't even begin to describe the feeling that spread over me. I felt alive, joyful, and... so whole. I tried to bring myself back to the reality of the National Gallery, Liz, and even Michael. But none of it mattered anymore, except the reality of the nearness of this glorious man sitting beside me.

He WAS the man in the painting and my dreams!

What's more I knew I had loved him aeons ago.

This incredible realisation addled my brain. I was totally lost as I thought of the implications involved in this meeting of hearts, minds and... long-lost... centuries old LOVE.

A name forced its way into my brain. 'It's Anthony... it's my dearest Anthony!'

I sat up straight, and tried to close my mind to what was happening. I don't believe in reincarnation, or anything remotely like that. The whole thing is fanciful and ridiculous. I closed my eyes to see if this scene of renewal would suddenly disappear.

But it didn't.

'Yes, I was really there,' he repeated, his voice was gentle, yet persuasive. 'And so were you.'

'I was?' I turned round to look at him again. Confusion... improbability... and even denial spread through my mind, as I continued to try to deny the inevitable.

'Yes,' he said. 'You painted this picture, and afterwards you fell into my arms each night. You must remember our lives together.'

'I painted this picture? But...'

'Will this help you to remember?' From inside his jacket he produced a little white flower, which was bruised, but to me it was instantly identifiable. He pressed it into my hands, leant over and kissed me. 'My sweetest Rebecca. I've waited so, so long for you... I thought I had lost you in the mists of time.'

I stared at the flower, and all my doubts evaporated in an explosion of recognition. I remembered the wonderful love we shared so long ago. 'You called me Rebecca. Yes, I remember now. You gave me a flower at the end of each sitting. Anthony, how could I have forgotten?'

'Our time has come, my sweetest Rebecca. The sands of time have decreed that we must meet again. Our love has been too strong.'

'Yes, Anthony. Our time has indeed come. I too have been waiting for you... but in my dreams... always in my dreams.'

'Our dreams have now become a reality, my sweet one.' He took my hand, and pulled me slowly towards him.

My heart pounded as we embraced.

My memory seemed to be searching far back in time, until I remembered the last time we were together. 'Anthony, my beloved; we've found one another again.' His touch felt like every delicious feeling I had ever known before.

'Come with me, Rebecca,' he pleaded.

'I will follow you for ever,' I whispered gently.

Where were we going? I didn't know and I didn't care. So, forsaking all else, I was Anthony's devoted and willing slave, and I followed him.

TEMPTATION

It was Monday lunchtime, and James Underwood was sitting drinking a cup of coffee in the café opposite the bank where he'd worked for the last ten years…

…and he was playing a dangerous waiting game.

For the first time in many months, James felt intensely excited. He believed that if he did nothing and told no one, financial security would fall neatly into his lap. He had the chance of a better future firmly within his grasp, as long as he could put his plan into action. If it worked, then and only then, could he persuade his wife, Alison, to come back to him. James loved her desperately, and missed her more and more each day. He knew he would do anything to get her and his son Jason back.

He was sitting at his usual table, and the intense aroma from his cup of strong, black coffee, helped to clear his head, but his hands betrayed his emotions; they were shaking as he placed the mug back on the table. He glanced up at the clock on the wall beside him. 'It's still only half-past one! How slowly time creeps by when you want it to go quickly,' he muttered to himself.

Beside his coffee cup was a packet of cigarettes, and James looked at it longingly. He really needed one, but he didn't fancy standing outside in the heavy rain he could see bouncing up from the ground outside. In his mind's eye he could see the computer sitting on the desk in his office in the building opposite. It was waiting for him. He could also see the names and figures on the screen; they were so clear, that he could almost see them flickering. His whole body began to shake when he realised the enormity of what he was planning to do. He closed his eyes. Could he really go through with this? A vision of his wife Alison's face appeared before him, and he knew he had no alternative if he was ever to get his family back together again.

James had just celebrated his 38th birthday alone. Alison had left him a year ago today, and had taken his pride and joy, his five-year old son, Jason with her. At first, he'd felt angry and bitter, and hated her with such venom that it had surprised him. He was normally such a kind, patient person and was never quick to condemn anyone. But as the lonely months passed by, his financial worries had intensified. He had to admit that, despite her betrayal, he had an unstoppable longing to have Alison and Jason back beside him again.

With these thoughts burning inside him, he pushed a lock of light brown hair out of his eyes, and continued to stare at the entrance to the bank. Not even the passing traffic could interfere with his gaze: it was intense and unswayable. He was totally broke. He knew that the bank held the key to his future, and he had to be quite sure that his plan would work.

The events that had led up to this new-found, but dangerous optimism, kept going round and round in his brain…

It had all started last Friday evening.

James had been about to close his computer down for the weekend, when he decided to check his salary for the month. It rarely changed, but sometimes the tax varied for some reason, and December had for obvious reasons, been an expensive month. He clicked onto the salaries file, and then scrolled downwards until his name appeared.

He closed his eyes in exasperation, when he noticed that a mistake had been made, and he didn't have enough time or the energy, to change it. He closed the file and switched off his desktop. James had a busy weekend ahead of him, and he managed to put it to the back of his mind as he left the office.

James woke up early on Saturday morning, and looked at the clock beside his bed; it was only 4.30 a.m., and still dark outside. Something was niggling away in his mind, and he sat up straight. When he was reading the salaries list yesterday, did he really see the wrong figure beside his name, or was it just wishful thinking? He was feeling tired at the time, and still was, but yes, he was pretty sure the figures were wrong: they were much too high! This continued to bother him, and when Alison's face floated into his mind again, an idea came to him in a flash. If the incorrect sum was ignored, it would, unless it was changed, be automatically credited to his account. Surely nobody would know if he let it slip through? Adrenaline flowed through his body at the thought of all that money. These thoughts continued to fill him with excited anticipation, and prevented any possibility of further sleep.

James spent the rest of the weekend in a state of unease, and arrived at the bank early on Monday morning. He was still not sure whether his memory was serving him correctly or not. Perhaps he'd imagined it, because he was under a great deal of pressure, and he did forget things sometimes? All he knew was that he had to find out the truth. He ran up to his office on the first floor two steps at a time, and almost collided with one of the office cleaners as he turned a corner.

'Oh, Mr. Underwood. You did make me jump,' she said with a flustered grin. 'You're an early bird and no mistake; it's only 8 o'clock. Can't you keep away?'

'It would seem not, Mrs. Bradley,' James replied breathlessly, with only the tiniest grimace of a smile. As he walked towards his office he couldn't help worrying about bumping into one of the biggest gossips in the bank. He would have to be careful from now on.

Once he was in his office, he switched his computer on,

and it whirred into obedient life. Placing his legs untidily beneath his desk, he began to move the mouse around on its pad, clicking expertly… until a list of names appeared.

A frisson of excitement passed over him as he scrolled through the list, until he found the entry he was looking for… and his body stiffened.

'Yes, there's my name, "**James Underwood**" and… and next to it, the enormous figure of "**£21,500.00**".' His heart began to race: he hadn't imagined it after all. He knew perfectly well that the figure should have read "**£2,150.00**", and he should change it, but in his present state of mind, the correct procedure was about to be thrown out of the window. His heartbeat accelerated wildly. Paula, the girl who was responsible for doing the salaries each month had been feeling unwell and hadn't noticed the error. A hand seemed to be holding his heart in a vice as he stared at the screen.

'Good morning, James.' A man's voice cut into his thoughts, and this time his heart leapt within his chest. 'It's nice to see you at your desk so early. Did you have a good weekend?' the voice continued.

James turned round to see the bank manager, Brian Abbott standing in the doorway.

'Er… yes, good morning, Mr. Abbott, sir,' he managed to blurt out. He desperately tried not to let his agitation show. 'I did have a good weekend, thank you.' Liar, he thought. You had a perfectly miserable time. You had Jason to look after, and the weather had been really bad. Neither of you had enjoyed it, because your mind was on other more pressing matters.

'Don't forget that on top of your usual duties, you have to do the salaries at the end of the day. Paula Hadderton has the 'flu and I'm afraid she won't be in the office for several more days. I must say she didn't look at all well on Friday. Well, I must get on… busy, busy day as usual.'

'There's a lot of it about,' James called out as his boss walked towards his office door. James had been sweating profusely, and was hoping that Mr. Abbott hadn't noticed.

Throughout the morning, he tried to carry out his normal duties, but his mind kept returning to that figure beside his name. He'd hardly been able to contain himself. To James, the sum of £21,500 was a large amount of money, and once it was transferred into his account he would be able to pay off most of his debts. And more importantly, Alison might come back to him. He could then buy Jason the little bicycle he wanted, and then he might feel proud of him again.

James realised that his brain was racing ahead of him, and he took a deep breath. At that moment, a little voice impinged itself into the innermost part of his brain.

How could your son, be proud of someone who steals from a bank? But James ignored it. Instead he had a vision…

He could see Alison standing in a brightly lit tunnel. She was holding Jason's hand and walking toward him…

Suddenly James knew that if had any hope of getting his family back together again, then he had to go through with his plan. He would be a fool not to, and besides, he might never get the chance again. The normal office procedure was to leave the employees' salaries until the end of the day's business. It was sheer torture for him to have to wait so long, but he'd only one alternative and that was to sit it out. Lunchtime eventually arrived and trying to act normally, he crossed the narrow street to the cafe.

The memory of the last few days diminished as he looked at his watch. 'I've another two or more hours left before I can put my plan into action,' he said under his breath. But his agitated thoughts wouldn't let him remain in the here and now for long. It drifted even further back to that painful, fateful day twelve months earlier, when Alison had decided to leave him.

He remembered that she'd been spoiling for a fight all evening, She'd practically thrown his dinner on the table, and then complained bitterly when he hadn't eaten it all.

'That's typical of you,' she said. 'You never do anything properly, do you? You have no drive, no ambition and no bloody appetite either. Jason needs some new clothes and shoes, and so do I.' Alison took a deep breath before continuing to goad him. 'And just in case you haven't noticed, this place needs decorating too. But you... you always take the easy route. You do nothing. Well, I've just about had enough. I'm leaving you.'

Alison's words tipped James into the depths of despair, as she continued. 'I can't take any more. I'm going to live with Mathew Taylor: we've been seeing one another for some time. He's something big in the city, he drives an expensive red sports car, and he's easily able to offer me and Jason anything we want.'

Tears began to form in his eyes as he recalled Alison's unfeeling, spiteful words. But on the other hand, he knew that she'd been right. He was spineless. And what had he done to try to get her back up until now? Nothing! Total inertia had taken over his mind. He'd been numbed by it all.

James knew that he couldn't stand the ignominy of only being allowed to see Jason each weekend much longer either. The courts had given him reasonable access. Reasonable access for whom, he asked himself miserably? He also knew that his young son was growing away from him. Jason was always talking about Matthew whenever he took him out for the day. He buried his head in his hands. If he hadn't dug himself into such a deep financial hole two years ago, he wouldn't have had to go to a "loan shark" in the first place, and that had been the start of all his problems. The amount of money he owed had doubled, and he'd become a sad, depressed, lonely person. Was there any wonder that Alison had left him?

'Would you like some more coffee, Mr. Underwood?' a girl's voice enquired, rapidly bringing him back to the present again.

'No… no thank you, Susie,' he replied looking at his watch. 'I ought to be getting back to the bank, so could I have the bill please?'

'Yes of course. You had two cups of coffee so that will be £3.00 please.' James handed her the correct money. 'Thank you,' she said looking at him. 'You didn't have any sandwiches today. Are you feeling O.K?'

'Yes… yes, I'm fine. I'm just not very hungry, that's all.'

'See you tomorrow, then?' Susie said brightly, picking up his coffee mug. 'Do take care.'

James walked out into the street, crossed the road, and made his way into the bank. He spent the next two hours in an agony of suspense. He continued to argue with himself about the consequences of not changing the inaccurate salary against his name. But his desire to get his family back was his main priority.

Once the bank was closed to the public, he accessed the salary file, and he worked steadily through the list until he reached his own name. James stared at the figure beside it, and his heart raced. His fingers began to shake, as he hesitated over the keys, and indecision gripped him by the throat. 'Can I actually go through with it?' he asked himself. 'What will happen if and when they discover that I embezzled the bank out of so much money?'

The telephone beside him rang shrilly, and he swore to himself as he lifted the receiver.

'Hello James Underwood here. How can I help you?' He tried to keep the mounting hysteria out of his voice.

'James,' a woman's voice croaked. 'It's Paula here. Have you done the salaries yet? Only I made a mistake on Friday, and forgot to alter it. I had a temperature, and I felt so ill that I had to leave early. I've only just remembered.'

His heart missed a beat. He was silent for a moment.

'James, are you still there?'

'Yes, I am. I'm sorry. I dropped some papers on the floor, and had to pick them up.' He cleared his throat, and tried to make his voice sound normal. 'As a matter of fact I was just about to phone you. I had of course discovered the error, and I was about to put in the correct sum.' He'd lied again, he thought, and his shoulders began to sag. He forced a laugh. 'Not that that sort of figure wouldn't have come in handy, Paula.'

Paula gave a croaky laugh. 'Yes we'd all love that kind of salary wouldn't we? Anyway, thank you for doing that, James. I'm so relieved. It's not the first time I've made that sort of mistake, and if Mr. Abbott had found out, I probably would have been in real trouble. Thanks again. You're a real friend.'

'Think nothing of it, Paula. I'm glad I was able to help. I hope you feel better soon. Bye.'

James replaced the receiver feeling small, but grateful. Paula had prevented him from doing something incredibly stupid. How could he have even thought of doing such a thing? He could never have got away with it, and he shivered violently. If only thinking about committing a crime made him a thief, then he was one, and he deserved the maximum punishment – even if it was only punishment inflicted upon himself.

He took a deep breath... and keyed in his correct salary.

His spirits plummeted. He wanted Alison and Jason

back so badly. There was no denying the fact the extra money would have been a godsend, but it wasn't meant to be. Somehow he managed to complete the list, and checked it thoroughly.

James felt sick with disgust and guilt, as he cleared his desk at the end of the day. He left the bank and drove his old, battered Morris Minor slowly back to his empty house. He knew he should eat something, but he didn't feel at all hungry. There wasn't much food in the cupboard anyway, as he'd forgotten to do the shopping at the weekend. Instead, he made himself a cup of coffee, and sat miserably in front of the television.

Later, James was still castigating himself for even thinking about not rectifying Paula's typing error, when the sound of the front door bell made him jump. 'It's nearly ten o'clock, and I'm not expecting anyone.' He walked out into the hall, and peered through the little glass spyhole in the door.

It seemed just like a tunnel, and his stomach churned.

Alison and little Jason were standing in the shining light from the bare bulb above their heads. He couldn't believe what he was seeing; his earlier vision had come true! It had been raining hard, and they were both very wet as if they'd been walking for some time. Alison looked so unhappy, and his heart melted as he opened the door.

'Hello, James,' she said, her eyes glistening with emotion. 'Do you think we could come in, please?' Alison's battered old suitcase, complete with the tattered remnants of stickers and pennants from long forgotten places, sat forlornly beside her on the tiled surface of the porch. She picked it up.

'Yes, come in both of you. You're soaked... and let me take that case. It looks heavy.'

'Thank you James. I... I don't know what to say.'

An awkward silence descended upon them.

James couldn't believe what was happening, and he eventually stuttered his reply. 'I'm afraid that the house is not very tidy, but I... I...' They were like two strangers as they stared at one another. Jason stood silently between them, constantly looking up from one to the other for reassurance. His large brown eyes were brimming over with tears.

'James,' Alison blurted out. 'I've left Matthew.'

'You've left him, but why?' was all he could think of saying.

'I couldn't put up with his violent moods any longer.' Tears began to trickle down her face. 'You see he was always getting drunk and... into debt.'

'And debt is what I know a lot about, Alison,' he replied grimly.

'I know you got yourself into debt, James, but at least you weren't violent, or... dishonest.'

'Dishonest?' He felt his face going red.

'Yes. Matthew is appearing in court tomorrow morning. He has apparently embezzled a large amount of money from his company over the past three years, so that explains the reason for his expensive lifestyle. Can you imagine it? I couldn't live with someone who's done that kind of thing. Please will you have us back, James?'

'I don't know what to say, Alison. I'm still in debt and I can't offer you much, but I still have my job at the bank, thank heavens. And,' he added in a strained, quiet voice, 'I still love you despite everything.' He stared at them, hardly daring to breathe, in case they disappeared again. 'I've missed you so much. Of course I'll have you back.'

'James, I love you too. I'm so sorry that I didn't realise it before. I don't care about having lots of money anymore. Having money didn't make Matthew and me happy. Now

105

that Jason's at school, I've found myself a little job. The pay isn't that bad, and with your salary at the bank, I'm sure we can manage. What do you think?'

'Yes, yes, yes. Alison. I know we will manage.' He looked at her worried face. 'I've learnt an extremely important lesson today.'

'Oh yes, what was that?'

'Alison... I...' He hesitated and a smile spread over his face. 'It's nothing important really... I'll tell you about it one day. Welcome home, my darling.'

CURVED PATHWAYS

It's such a beautifully bright, sunny day, and how I wish I could go outside into the world again, or meet some friends for lunch, or go to the pub… but I can't. I have to sit here and watch the world go by without me. Every day come rain or shine, I just sit here waiting for the postman to arrive.

Ah, here he is at last. Mmm, he must be new to the round because I don't recognise him, and why has he stopped? WOW, he's quite good-looking from this distance. Young and slim and his hair is hanging right down over his forehead, just like Neil's used to, and he's got a cheeky smile… *Nicola Forsythe, behave yourself. Deep down, you know that someone like him is way beyond your league,* a little voice inside my head is insisting.

'I know… I know… he wouldn't look twice at someone like me, who is forced to sit in a wheelchair all day. Ooh these windows do need cleaning, and the curtains need a good wash. If only I could do them myself.

Ah, he's sorting through his bag… and now he's opening the gate. Thank goodness he's got some letters for me. Come on please hurry. No, he's stopped again and he's looking around. Walk up the path to the door, please? I know it's a curved and twisted path, but it's a beautiful one. Yes, I knew it. He's admiring the trees, and the acer-palmatum, the two butterfly bushes, and the weeping willow, with its dainty branches gently dipping into the tiny pond. It's such a peaceful scene, so I can't blame him for looking.

The pathway to my door meanders and twists just like a stream, before passing under a rustic archway over which climb a profusion of roses and clematis. I'm so proud of it. Not that I'm in any fit state to tend it, of course. I always position my wheelchair by the window, so that I can see all the comings and goings at the pond. It helps keep me sane, as

I feel like an old person sometimes. Look at me. My legs are still part of me, but they don't work… and never will now.

Thank goodness, I can get some help with the gardening, otherwise it would all look like a jungle. But how much longer can I afford to keep paying out for its upkeep? I can only just afford to pay the gardener, and Mrs. Bolton, bless her; at least the housework is taken care of. I mourn for the days when I could walk out into the garden, and dig my fingers into the cool, soft earth. It always gave me such an extra special feeling: a feeling that I was actually part of creation. Friends used to say that I had green fingers, as plants always obeyed my will, and grew tall and strong. But not so now, although my one consolation is that I can enjoy watching someone else doing it for me.

How I wish Neil could be with me to watch everything grow. He used to love the garden. I'm expecting an important letter from the Compensation Board, or whatever it is called nowadays. They've already pronounced upon a verdict, and I don't yet know what that is. My heart always pounds like a drum, when the postman is due.

Oh no, he's stopping again, and is looking down at the pond. Perhaps he can see one of the goldfish? Doesn't he realise that I desperately want to see what's in the letters he's holding in his hand? My twisting garden path is supposed to bring me good fortune, but instead it's filling my mind with worry and frustration. If only I could bang on the window to attract his attention. Good he's looking this way at last, and he's walking under the arch. In a few minutes I will know.

Suddenly I feel horribly dizzy, as if I'm in a dream. Oh I don't believe it… the pictures are starting again…

Horrific pictures of the accident are once more crowding and insinuating themselves into my mind; please not now, go away… please go away. Too late! I can see the crazy look on the terrified face of the man driving the car…

his eyes are staring full of desperation and fear through his windscreen. We both know he's going to hit us. There's nothing we can do… there's a loud squeal of brakes!

I can hear two people screaming: one voice is mine… and the other… the voice of my husband, Neil as he dies! The pictures are all melting into one… and I close my eyes…

I hear the sound of the metal cover on the letter box clang as the postman puts the letters in. There's nothing wrong with my hearing, because I hear them fall on to the door mat. I sigh, and wonder if anyone has remembered that it's my 40th birthday today. Quickly I must get out into the hall. Damn this chair, it's so slow. Yes, there are one, two, three, four birthday cards as far as I can see.

Ah, it looks like the letter I've been waiting for at last, and my heart is thumping wildly. It takes a few moments while I position my wheelchair so that I can reach the letters. Damn my useless legs and shaking fingers. Don't worry about tearing the envelope, because it's the contents that are important.

My eyes mist over…

"Dear Mrs. Forsythe,
The Board has much pleasure in announcing that you are due to receive the sum of £500,000 (Five hundred thousand pounds) in compensation for the accident eighteen months ago, in which your husband died, and you received severe life changing injuries. We…"

I can't read the rest because of the tears in my eyes. £500,000 to compensate for the loss of a husband and a normal life!

But, realisation dawns… my chi… my cosmic energy… my twisted pathway… my saviour… I can now afford to stay here!

SECOND CHOICES

The clouds in the early morning sky rumbled and grumbled their way eastwards, as Betty Westwood, with her umbrella firmly held up against the elements, hurried her way along the footpath. She looked up at the sky: she hated storms. A streak of forked lightning, followed almost instantaneously by another loud clap of thunder, forced its way across the darkened sky. The rain was incessant.

'Good morning, Mrs. Westwood. Lovely weather,' the postman said as he ambled by carrying his usual heavy load. He looked cheerful even though rainwater was running like a torrent from his hat and cape.

'Yes. Good morning. It's going to clear up later so they say,' she said as she hurried along.

'If you believe that, then you'll believe anything.' He pointed to his boots with a chuckle. 'I'm thinking of swapping these for a pair of flippers!'

Betty laughed at the thought of a postman wearing flippers, crossed the street and hurried the remaining few yards to her shop. It was bad enough being a Monday morning, but a Monday morning combined with a near tropical downpour, was something else.

It was just before 9 o'clock and apart from the postman, and one solitary shopper, the high street was empty. Betty glanced upwards at the blue and gold sign above the shop, which read **"SECOND CHOICES"**. Despite the rain, she sighed with pleasure. The sight of her little second hand clothes shop, tightly sandwiched between a small upmarket art gallery, and a fashionable but expensive designer dress shop, never failed to please her. She took great delight in telling her friends that her shop was like a rose between two thorns, but never the other way round of course.

Betty had started up the business just over eighteen

months earlier, and it was doing quite well. She felt proud that she was now able to buy a few of her own clothes from the dress shop next door! She enjoyed her work and a buzz of excitement always flowed through her when she arrived each morning. Betty lived alone, and consequently loved meeting and talking to her customers. She smiled as she wondered what challenges today would bring.

Once inside, she turned the notice on the door from "CLOSED" to "OPEN". Several letters were lying on the mat, and she quickly thumbed her way through them, but there was nothing of much interest… just a few bills. Betty Westwood was an attractively slim, elegant woman in her late forties, divorced, but not at all unhappy about it.

Before she'd even had time to switch on the lights, the antique bell above the door jangled loudly. A woman walked in carrying a plastic bag and a large golfing umbrella. She seemed to be holding the weight of the world upon her slender shoulders, and as she looked around the shop, she reminded Betty of a rather frightened rabbit.

'Good morning madam. How can I help you?' Betty asked. There was no reply. The woman obviously had a lot on her mind, she thought, as she was looking around the shop almost as if she was expecting someone to jump out at her.

Betty studied her. People fascinated her, and she prided herself on the fact that she could sum everyone up at first glance. This woman had a kind of faded beauty, and as she pushed her straight blond-to-grey hair behind her ears, her hands trembled slightly. Her clothes looked expensive and probably designer labelled. They were the sort of clothes sold by the shop next door. Perhaps she'd wandered into SECOND CHOICES by mistake, Betty thought as she tried to smother a smile. She was also sure that she'd seen her somewhere before too, but where? Then she remembered.

111

The woman's name was Appleton, and she lived in one of the large detached houses at the end of the high street.

'Good morning, madam. Can I help you?' Betty repeated.

Mrs. Appleton was nervously twisting the handles of the bag around her fingers. 'I... I'm not really sure,' she said, jumping at the sound of Betty's voice. She sounded cultured, but hesitant. 'I... I was wondering if you could find a home... for these.' She tipped the contents of the bag out on to the counter.

Betty couldn't believe her eyes!

Before her lay some of the sauciest and brightest underwear she'd ever seen. There were bright red, frilly bras and knickers, red and black boned corsets with garters to match and even, Betty noted with some surprise, some exotic G-strings! She couldn't help wondering if Mrs. Appleton had ever actually worn any of them. She didn't look the type.

Betty picked one up between her finger and thumb and examined it. 'I'm really sorry, madam but I'm not sure that I'll be able to sell these. Where did you get them?' she said, at last taking off her damp coat, and placing it on the chair beside her.

Mrs. Appleton turned the colour of her unwanted underwear. 'Please take them,' she said. 'I don't want to throw them away because I'm sure they were expensive, and it would be a dreadful waste. But if... if my husband were to find them, I... I don't know what would happen. He can be dreadfully jealous you see and wouldn't understand. They... they were all gi... gifts from a friend of mine.' Embarrassed tears began to gather in the corners of her eyes, 'I don't want anything for them,' she said as her voice trailed to a whisper. 'So perhaps you could give the money they raise to charity or something?'

Betty didn't quite know what to say or do, because she'd never had to face a situation like this before. A mixture of embarrassment and sheer nosiness began to fill her mind.

'Well madam, I'll certainly try to sell them, but we don't get much call for this type of clothing.'

'Oh dear, and I was so hoping that I could be rid of them.'

Almost as soon as the words had been uttered, the doorbell jangled again, and a middle-aged man walked in. Mrs. Appleton tried to hide all the underwear, but it was too late, and with a look of sheer pleasure on his face, the man made a beeline for them. She suddenly rushed to the other side of the shop, obviously wishing to get as far away from the incriminating articles as possible.

'Ah,' the delighted man said, 'this must be my lucky day.' With great relish he picked up an outrageous red and black boned bra, and held it up against himself. 'Do you know, I can't believe this? They're exactly what I'm looking for.' He began to search through the other items, and then noticed that Betty was staring at him. 'Oh, please excuse me. Good morning. My name's Jones, Howard Jones. How do you do?'

Betty realised that her mouth was open, and she closed it instantly. 'Good morning to you. Can I be of any assistance?' she said, trying to flatten out a grin. Surely, she thought, this man wasn't thinking of buying this saucy underwear for himself?

'Yes, I think you can,' he replied. 'These really are quite something aren't they?'

'They are extremely... er... pretty and were you thinking of buying something like this for your wife perhaps, sir?'

'Why no, they're for me actually,' he said giving a wicked grin. 'Do you think they'll fit?' He held up a pair of

113

red and black knickers with fur around the edge. Betty wasn't quite sure whether he was teasing her or not when, with his eyes twinkling mischievously, he held up first one visual delight after another.

Mr. Jones was just reaching for another red and black bra, when a woman walked into the shop and stood beside him at the counter. Betty smiled at her. 'Good morning madam, I won't keep you a moment.'

'That's O.K, we're together. I'm his wife,' she said with a broad and knowing grin.

Howard Jones was in his element as he continued to rummage through the underwear. He turned to speak to his wife. 'Darling, look what I've found? Is the colour right?'

'Yes dear, they're all perfect, but don't you think they're a little small for you?'

'Well, if what I've heard is true, David Watson rather likes this sort of thing,' he whispered trailing his voice seductively. 'I'd say they were just right.' He turned to Betty. 'How much would you like for them?'

Whilst all this had been going on, Mrs. Appleton had been hiding behind a rail full of clothes. She felt terrified. Her heart was beating violently in her chest and she felt the first stirrings of nausea. 'Oh my God, no,' she whispered, 'he knows David!'

As if on cue, a loud clap of thunder rattled all the windows.

'What if he wants to buy all the underwear, and supposing David finds out and recognises them; what on earth will he think? Why oh why did I come in here? After all, I could have just thrown them in the dustbin. Ohhh…'
She raced headlong out of the shop and into the storm.

Betty was momentarily distracted by Mrs. Appleton's sudden departure. 'I'm sorry, what were you saying?'

Mr. Jones smiled at her. 'I would like to know how much you want for them.'

'Will you be requiring all of them, sir?'

'Yes please. I can't believe it. They are all exactly what I want.'

'I don't really know, as I don't usually sell this kind of thing. Do you think that £15.00 would be too much?' Betty's need to laugh was becoming urgent.

He looked dubious. 'Mmmm... well...'

'£12.50 then?' she suggested, haggling for all she was worth.

'Erm...' He looked down at the underwear, and smiled again. 'Would you accept £10.00 for them?'

'Yes of course, I will. Thank you Mr. Jones, and to be honest with you, they only came in about ten minutes ago, and I'm glad that you've taking them off my hands. I hope you'll be very happy with them.'

'Oh I will, I will,' he said putting his hand in his pocket. 'Do you take debit cards, only I'm a bit short of cash at the moment?'

'I would prefer cash if you don't mind, Mr. Jones, and as I said, I don't usually sell this kind of clothing, so I'll be donating the £10 to a local charity.'

'I'll pay for them if you like, darling,' his wife said interrupting them. 'Otherwise you'll be late for the office.'

'OK thanks. I'll see you later darling.' He kissed his wife on the cheek, beamed at Betty and strode out of the shop.

Betty folded all the underwear and carefully placed them in one of her own blue and gold plastic "SECOND CHOICES" bags. By now, she was nearly fit to burst. Why should this quite ordinary looking man want to buy such obviously sexy female undergarments, and what's more, with his wife's encouragement? And what had this David

Watson person got to do with it? Oh well, there's no accounting for taste, she thought as she closed the bag. 'There you are Mrs. Jones. I hope your husband enjoys them.'

Mrs. Jones handed her a £10.00 note, and smiled a knowing smile. 'Oh he will… you can be sure of that.'

Betty could control herself no longer. 'Mrs. Jones,' she laughed, 'I know that it's none of my business, but… why…?'

'You really don't have to worry you know,' she said with a grin. 'David Watson is producing the Pantomime "Aladdin" in the Town Hall next week, and my husband is playing the part of "Wishee Washee". He actually needs all this… this underwear for his washing line! Thank you,' she said happily, and walked out of the shop.

Betty was left with her mouth wide open for the second time that day!

JUST CAUSE

'Come on then Sarah, don't leave me in suspense. What happened next?' The young woman sitting opposite Sarah Vernon leaned further towards her as she listened to her tale of woe. She was holding her wine glass daintily between well-manicured fingers, and gently swirling the pale liquid around the bowl. 'He didn't,' she said, 'what a hoot, do go on,' she entreated with a mischievous smile.

Sarah was not quite sure whether she was doing the right thing by confiding in her new found friend Rachael, because she seemed to be hanging on to her every word. But on the other hand, as they'd only met at a meeting of the local church Fund Raising Committee a couple of weeks ago, and Rachael didn't know any of the people involved, where was the harm? 'Yes,' she found herself replying. 'Can you believe it?'

'Yes, I can certainly believe it. Weddings, and marriage in particular, can be unpredictable things at the best of times,' Rachael replied, placing her glass neatly and precisely in the centre of a beer mat.

'You can say that again. I can laugh about it now, but at the time it was awful.' Sarah's laughter rang out like a bell, which was joined by the ancient church on the other side of the green as it struck two o'clock.

It was a beautifully sunny day, and a slight breeze ruffled the flowers in a vase on the table, thereby disturbing a rather persistent bumble bee. The Blue Boar Inn's colourful garden was filled with people all enjoying the warm summer sunshine. The sound of happy voices, together with the clink of glasses, floated around in the balmy breeze.

'Don't get me wrong, Rachael, I'm not at all sorry that it happened,' Sarah continued. Her large hazel eyes

117

suddenly flashed in anger. 'As far as I'm concerned, my friend Claire's intended, Alistair, was a dishonest, egotistical, disingenuous male chauvinist, who would think nothing of...'

'Can I take it then, that you didn't like this... this Alistair character very much?' Rachael quickly intervened.

'No I most certainly didn't.' Sarah was silent for a moment, as the memory of that disastrous day circled round and round in her mind.

'Penny for them?'

'Would you really give me a penny for my thoughts?' Sarah replied. 'Well they're not the most charitable thoughts in the world at the moment. Do you know it's the strangest thing, but I would never have put my brother Phillip down as a go-getter! He was always such a live and let live, kind of guy.'

Rachael smiled. 'Wow, I can picture it. The handsome knight on his white charger turning up outside the church just in the nick of time, to save his lady love from a fate worse than death. It sounds so deliciously romantic.'

'I couldn't believe what was happening,' Sarah said. She was now beginning to enjoy herself. 'You should have seen Alistair's face, he was absolutely furious. He must have seen his meal ticket disappearing into the sunset.'

'From that, can I assume that Claire's parents are quite wealthy?' Rachael said as she took a tissue out of her handbag.

'Not so as you'd notice,' Sarah said with a smile. 'The whole wedding thing must have cost an absolute fortune; it was five-star everything. Claire's father is a group chairman of a huge multi-national corporation somewhere in the City. He's the sort of person that the Shadow Chancellor of the Exchequer is always moaning about. When he receives a salary rise, everyone else has to go without.'

'Wow. That's definitely wealthy.' Rachael laughed as she picked up her glass, and drained the contents. 'Would you like another drink, and then perhaps you can tell me all the gory details? I really can't wait.'

'Yes please, but make it a small one this time.'

'Good. I won't be a minute.' She winked at Sarah as she stood up. 'I also want to have another look at that rather dishy man behind the bar. He looks a bit like Colin Firth, and as for his eyes...' Sarah watched her as she walked back into the old building. Rachael was slim, attractive, impeccably dressed, friendly and fun to be with. Sarah was impressed by her ability to listen, and to take an interest in what she was saying. So many people nowadays were superficial and only interested in talking about their own lives.

When Rachael walked back to the table a few minutes later, she wore an amused, quizzical expression on her face. 'I'll put him on hold for later,' she whispered devilishly.

Sarah laughed. 'By the way, there's a pond across the road, perhaps you should ask him to take a dip?' Sarah said. 'His name isn't Darcy by any chance, is it?'

Rachael giggled as she placed two glasses of sparkling wine on the table. 'We've obviously read the same books, or watched similar TV programmes in the past!'

'Obviously. Anyway thank you for the drink.'

'Now Sarah,' Rachael said out of the blue. 'I was just wondering how long your brother, and Claire had known one another. It must have come as a tremendous shock to you all when this man Alistair appeared on the scene.'

'Phillip and Claire had been seeing one another ever since they were at sixth-form college, and were thinking of moving in together. In fact, they'd even started to look for a flat to share. Everyone said that they were made for one another,' Sarah replied with a smile. 'Unfortunately, Phillip had to go to New York on business for a couple of months. Claire was at a bit of a loose end, and agreed to go to her firm's Christmas party. Of course, the inevitable happened. She was introduced to Alistair and found him… irresistible. He was tall, dark, extremely handsome, and managed to sweep Claire off her feet. We didn't know anything about it, until their wedding was announced.'

'How awful. That must have been a dreadful shock for everyone,' Rachael said.

'Yes it was. Phillip was devastated. In fact the whole family was extremely hurt and angry. But Claire and I were lifelong friends, and even though she'd dumped my brother for Alistair, I felt duty bound to go to the wedding. I didn't really want to go at all. I was completely torn.'

'The bastard,' Rachael said vehemently. Sarah blinked at her in surprise. 'Oh, I… I'm dreadfully sorry, Sarah. I didn't mean… and it's none of my business. I just feel so sorry for all of you. Weddings are usually such happy occasions, but this…'

'You needn't feel sorry for us at all. As far as the family is concerned, Claire had a lucky escape under the circumstances.' She tucked her long hair behind her ears, and removed her sunglasses. 'Right, you wanted to know exactly what happened, so I'll set the scene for you. When I come to think about it, the whole thing reminded me of a film I saw a few years ago. Are you sitting comfortably… then I'll begin.'

'Yes, it's such an intriguing story,' Rachael said excitedly.

'The church was simply bulging with people all dressed in their expensive finery. There were so many beautifully arranged flowers, all of which were colour coordinated of course, and the perfume was quite intoxicating.' Sarah stopped speaking and sipped her drink.

'Yes… and,' Rachael said eagerly leaning towards her once more.

'Well, you can picture it can't you? The elderly organist had finally got her teeth into the first chords of "Here Comes the Bride". Alistair, and the best man were waiting in front of the crowded pews and…' Sarah hesitated and took a deep breath.

'Don't stop now, please! Go on.'

'When Claire walked into the church with her father, there was an audible gasp of admiration from the congregation. She looked so beautiful. Eventually everyone settled down, and the wedding ceremony began. Everything went well, until the vicar asked if anyone knew of any just cause or impediment why these two people here present, should not be joined in holy matrimony, etc., when the door suddenly burst open and my brother, Phillip raced in. He was waving his arms around, and shouting something about stopping the ceremony. Then…' Sarah hesitated.

'Yes. What happened?'

'Well, poor Claire immediately burst into tears. As you can imagine, everyone was too shocked and stunned to do or say anything at first. I remember that there was an awkward silence, and then everyone started to speak at once. There was absolute mayhem for a while until the vicar managed to create some sort of order.'

Rachael lifted a beautifully curved eyebrow. 'Mmmm… and…?'

'Well,' Sarah continued, 'you don't expect that sort of thing to happen in real life, do you?' She stopped speaking, and sipped her drink.

'Come on don't keep me in suspense.'

'I noticed that Phillip was out of breath, and sweating as he ran up the aisle. Claire's father tried to grab hold of him, but my brother turned towards Alistair, and without

121

any warning, punched him. He stumbled, and tripped over a chair, with blood pouring from his nose.'

'Didn't your brother try to explain why he was so upset?'

'Yes. Phillip was wonderful. As he shouted for everyone to be quiet. I could see his whole body was shaking with anger, and he was gasping for breath. Anyway, he at last managed to speak.

"I'm sorry," he said, *"but I can't allow this... this mockery of a ceremony to continue."* There was another stunned silence. I tell you Rachael, my heart was pumping so wildly that I thought everyone could hear it. By this time of course, Alistair had managed to struggle to his feet, and was staggering towards my brother. Phillip immediately turned on him again saying, *"What's the matter Alistair, have we spoiled your fun?"*'

'My goodness, how dreadful,' Rachael said looking concerned.

'Alistair looked as if he was about to commit murder, and the best man had to fight hard to restrain him, which isn't normally listed among his wedding duties, is it? Nevertheless, he stood his ground and shouted at Phillip. *"What the hell do you think you're doing? You have no right."* At this stage, of course, the congregation seemed almost too stunned to think, or do anything.'

'I can't believe that this was all happening in a church, during a wedding. WOW!' Rachael said. 'What was Phillip's answer?'

'He just laughed in Alistair's face, and then blurted out... *"I... I have no right? What about you? For goodness sake man, you're already married. What about your wife?"* I remember hearing a loud scream, which I can only assume came from Claire, and another huge gasp from the congregation. It was all such a shock. Poor Claire, she was completely inconsolable.'

122

'I can only imagine how dreadful she was feeling.' Rachael was silent for a moment, and suddenly her pretty face darkened with anger. 'What was Alistair Currie's answer, Sarah? And more to the point, what did he say in his defence?' Her words were now cold and calculating.

Claire stared at her in amazement. 'What do you mean, Rachael?'

'I expect he grovelled and whined as usual.' Rachael immediately looked embarrassed, and covered her mouth with her hand. 'Oh dear, I'm so sorry, but...'

Sarah frowned. 'I don't understand, Rachael. Do you know Alistair then?'

'Yes, Sarah,' she replied looking contrite, 'I do. In fact, I know Alistair extremely well. I can honestly say that I had no idea what he was planning to do. It's bigamy and against the law, after all. You see, I found out through a mutual friend what he was intending to do, and she gave me Phillip's phone number. I was absolutely incensed by it all, ...and the rest you know.'

'So it was you who was responsible for...'

'Yes, and I'm so sorry for keeping my identity secret. You see my name is Rachael Currie. Unfortunately, Alistair is still my husband, even though he left me about a year ago. I feel that I must apologise to everyone involved. I'm so sorry about the subterfuge, but the divorce becomes final next week.'

Sarah was at a loss for words.

Rachel picked up her empty glass, stood up, smiled and said, 'Would you like another drink?'

AWAY TO ICELAND

Hannah Thompson sat in the crowded compartment feeling bored, and unhappy. She sighed. 'Not again, please, I'm getting so tired of this. It's the second time this week.' She sighed, and closed her eyes in exasperation. Her life wasn't going anywhere, and neither was the train. It was five minutes since the train had shuddered to a halt. Hannah could only assume that the train had broken down, or the driver was waiting for a red light to change to green. 'If only my life could be changed so easily,' she whispered to herself, hoping that her fellow passengers weren't listening.

Hannah worked as a clinical psychologist in a big London hospital, and spent all her time delving deeply into other people's confused minds. Consequently she had little time left at the end of the day to think about her own life. Today's problems had been difficult, to say the least. Despite her wide experience in treating patients with mental problems, one particular patient had displayed distinct suicidal tendencies. The hour-long consultation had left her feeling exhausted and inadequate. She felt unable to come to the correct diagnosis, and she finally referred him to one of her colleagues, Laura Anderson.

After looking through the file, Laura looked at her in such a way that Hannah felt like one of her patients, and she felt small and insignificant. 'Hannah,' Laura said with a sympathetic smile. 'What's the problem? It's a text-book diagnosis and, of course I'll take this patient on. But you are usually so good at these cases.'

'But...? There's always a but isn't there?' Hannah said quickly interrupting her. 'Look Laura, I'm not enjoying my work at the moment.' She could feel tears welling up in her eyes, and she looked away. 'I honestly don't know what's the matter with me.'

'I think I know what's wrong with you, Hannah. You need a holiday; a time away from this hospital. I feel like this sometimes myself. You need to get out more; meet people who don't have problems, and start enjoying yourself again. My diagnosis for you is to take a short break, and then you can come back to work with all your usual enthusiasm.'

'Thank you Laura, but I can't see how I can.'

'Hannah,' she replied placing her hand on top of hers. 'You and I know that you are an excellent psychologist, but even an expert needs to have some time away.'

Hannah walked away from her friend, in a haze of doubt and self-criticism. All she really wanted to do was to get home and put her feet up in front of the television, but she was stuck in a train which didn't appear to be going anywhere. There has to be more to life than this, she thought miserably. She sighed deeply, and shifted in her seat.

She looked at the passengers in her compartment. People had always fascinated her. A typical city-type angrily consulted his watch, and "tut-tutted" away to himself. Two elderly women on the other side of the carriage, actually began to speak to one another, which was quite unusual. Hannah couldn't hear the whole conversation, but little snippets wafted towards her, and she couldn't help smiling.

'Do you know, I had a lovely day shopping,' the woman was saying. 'There was this young man you see, and he...'

Really,' the other woman said eagerly. 'I've never heard of that before. Did you...' When they saw Hannah watching them, they put their heads together, and started whispering.

This relieved some of the tension Hannah could feel building up inside her. No wonder the English have a reputation for being standoffish, and cold; they only talked to one another in times of adversity, and sometimes not even then.

She yawned, and followed it with a sigh. She wasn't just bored with her profession – and this interminable journey, but her life in general. Hannah realised that she was obsessed with psychology; even her best friends were psychologists! After qualifying she'd found that she couldn't wait to put all her new found knowledge into practice. She quite rightly assumed that she had the prospect of an exciting career ahead of her, but somehow lately it had all gone sour. Perhaps being a psychologist wasn't the right career path for her anymore, she thought? So what else could she do with her life? Perhaps Laura is right, and I do need a holiday.

Why do you think you need a holiday? a little voice in her head enquired. 'Because I do that's all.' She realised with horror, that she'd said these words out loud. She looked around at the people sharing her compartment, but nobody moved, looked up, or even betrayed the fact that they might have heard her. They all continued to read their books, Kindles and newspapers as if nothing untoward had happened. What was wrong with them and why didn't they react to her sudden outburst, she wondered.

Hannah studied the man opposite. He was youngish, slightly balding and had a florid complexion. He also looked miserable, and probably had marital problems. An older man next to him was asleep and, unfortunately, his head was creeping ever closer to the young woman sitting on the other side. He was probably weary of having to make the same journey every day, just like her.

The young woman looked horrified, as his head finally came to rest on her shoulder. 'Please, please wake up,' she cried out. 'You're not at home, you're in a train for goodness sake.'

The man woke up with a start, and opened his eyes slowly. When he noticed what he was doing, he coughed, sat up straight, and looked around in embarrassment. 'I'm... I'm really sorry. Pl... please forgive me,' he stuttered as he tried to regain some dignity. He shook his newspaper, and pretended to read it as if nothing had happened.

Hannah couldn't resist a slight giggle, and tried to cover it up by looking at her watch. The train had been stationary now for thirty-five minutes, and some of the other passengers were starting to become agitated. She turned to her own newspaper and scanned the holiday pages. There were so many places in the world to see. 'I could go on a tour of the Greek Islands, or Bali, or the Caribbean, she thought. In fact a cruise in the Caribbean might be fun, and far better than looking at the dingy old apartment buildings she could see through the window. They'd been built far too close to the railway, with no thought of the well-being of their occupants in mind. To make matters worse, it was pouring with rain, and Hannah watched as the water cascaded in separate streams down the dirty window.

She turned her mind back to thoughts of a holiday. Laura was right. Going on holiday would do her a lot of good. But who could she go with, because she didn't fancy going by herself? Her closest friend Susan had already decided to go away with her live-in boyfriend, and anyway, they were only interested in looking at boring temples. Once upon a time that sort of holiday would have appealed to her, but not now.

Hannah started to think that life was passing her by. She was nearly thirty, and people told her that she was attractive. But where had it got her? She wore her shoulder length brown hair straight, in a Mary Quant style, which really suited her. Her eyes had an open and friendly appeal,

127

which usually paid dividends when she was examining patients. She enjoyed the company of most of her men friends, but would she ever consider spending the rest of her life with any of them? The answer had to be a big 'NO'. Until recently she'd been happy to go on various courses to further her career, but now she considered that there had to be more to life than the academic merry-go-round on which she'd found herself.

An item in the small adverts column of her newspaper aroused her interest.

"Enthusiastic single travellers wanted to join a team of people going to Iceland. Only those with a good sense of humour need apply. Please contact Jeremy Cranford-Browne"

It listed a telephone number in London.

After a few jerky movements, the train started moving again, and the depressing old apartment buildings disappeared from view. Iceland, she thought. That would be a challenge, but was she an enthusiastic traveller, and what's more to the point, did she possess a good sense of humour? She tussled with the idea, and then read it again. The whole concept was appealing, and she put a little cross against it for future reference.

The train eventually arrived at her station nearly forty-five minutes late and she hurried home in the driving rain. When she walked into her flat she was surprised that it suddenly felt so cold and unwelcoming. She'd never felt like this before but after eating an unappetising microwave meal, she remembered the holiday advert. After reading it through a couple of times, she decided that it could possibly give her the impetus she needed, and without stopping to think further, she tapped in the number.

'Hello, Jeremy Cranford-Browne here. Can I help you?' He sounded cultured and his voice was deep and friendly.

'Yes, I certainly hope so,' Hannah said taking a deep breath. 'I... I've just seen your advertisement in the evening paper. I was wondering if you could tell me something about your proposed trip to Iceland. It sounds as if it could be great fun.'

'Well, I'm not really sure that it's still on.' He sounded really disappointed. 'You see the people who originally said they would come with me have cried off, and you're the only person who has shown any interest since then.'

'Oh, I'm sorry. In that case, I'll...'

'No... no, please don't hang up,' he said. 'Perhaps we could meet to discuss it? And do you know anyone else who might be interested?'

'No sorry, I can't think of anyone off-hand.' Hannah knew she was going to like this gently spoken man with the persuasive voice.

'Well that won't matter, will it? Yes, why don't we meet to discuss it? I'm free most evenings. What about you?'

'Yes, so am I.' Hannah replied.

'Can you make tomorrow night?' he said, sounding hopeful.

'Yes, I can. Where shall we meet?' There was a moment's awkward silence.

'Why don't we meet at Waterloo station under the clock,' they chorused. They both laughed.

'I'm afraid that I don't even know your name,' Jeremy said, 'I really would like to know.'

'It's Hannah, Hannah Thompson.'

'Well Hannah. How about tomorrow evening at 7.30 p.m. underneath the clock at Waterloo Station?'

'Yes, that sounds wonderful, Jeremy. I'll see you there.' Hannah hesitated, and then laughed. 'How will I recognise you? It's a very popular meeting place. I've heard from other people, that the space under the clock is often quite crowded.'

'I'll be wearing a red rose in my button-hole, and...' he paused for a moment, 'and another one between my teeth,' he said. 'I think that's what people usually do. Well perhaps not many people would have a rose between their teeth, but I'm sure you'll have no difficulty picking me out. I'm six feet four inches tall, with light brown curly hair. I wear glasses and I'll be wearing a light brown trench coat. That's enough about me. How will I recognise you, Hannah?'

'I can't think how to describe myself. I've got longish brown hair and blue-to-grey eyes, and I suppose I'm reasonably slim. In fact there's nothing remarkable about me at all. I'm of medium height... and I don't wear glasses,' she added as an afterthought.

'Hannah, that sounds really good to me, and I can't wait to meet you. Just wear a deep red rose in your brown hair, and I won't fail to recognise you. I'm really looking forward to seeing you tomorrow. Bye.'

'Me too. Bye Jeremy.'

At 7.20 p.m. the following evening, Hannah stood under the famous Waterloo Station clock, looking anxiously at every passerby, and wondering whether she should have come. She knew nothing at all about Jeremy Cranford-Browne, and doing something on the spur of the moment was completely alien to her. But she needed to be free of all the constraints that her job placed upon her. This was her bid for freedom. She now sought the wide open spaces of her imagined brave, new and exciting world.

The clock above her head, struck 7.30 p.m. and Hannah began to panic. 'Is he going to come?' Then she saw someone who fitted his description, and her heart thumped in her chest. Yes, he was wearing a red rose, and he did stand out amongst the crowd. She nervously patted the one she'd carefully placed in her hair. She looked at him as he approached the clock, and felt slightly disappointed when she saw that he didn't have a rose between his teeth! But the moment he saw her, he took a long red rose from within his coat and placed it horizontally in his mouth.

Suddenly Jeremy was by her side and looking down at her. Hannah thought that he had a really wonderful smile, and her heart began to race. He took the rose out of his mouth, and handed it to her.

'Thank you, it's beautiful,' she said. 'You are Jeremy, aren't you?'

'Yes,' he answered, hardly able to take his eyes from her face, 'and you have to be Hannah. Hello.'

'Yes, I am. Hello.' Hannah felt confused. She was used to looking into people's eyes to try to assess how they were feeling, but his had the most unnerving effect upon her. He reached for her hand, and his gentle touch made her feel warm inside.

'Do you know, you're exactly as I'd pictured you.' Jeremy gripped her hand more firmly and steered her gently towards the station's exit. 'My car is in the road outside, and now that we've met, where would you like to go? May I suggest dinner because I'm starving?'

'Yes… yes dinner would be lovely.' For once Hannah was completely at a loss for words.

'I'm sorry to have to rush you,' Jeremy said, 'but I'm parked on a double yellow line, and I saw a traffic warden just before I came in here.' They walked through the big archway and out into the brilliant evening sunshine. Fortunately the warden was busy writing a ticket for another motorist. 'Ah, I think I got away with it this time,' he said as he strode towards a vintage green sports car. 'Here she is.'

'Is this one yours, Jeremy? It's a beautiful car,' Hannah said as she stared at it.

'Yes, it is. It's a Bugatti, and I call her "The Bug",' he said as he opened the door for her. He squeezed his long legs into the car, and turned to her. 'The Bug is my one luxury, and I hope you like her.'

'Jeremy, she's absolutely wonderful. I have to say that I've never been in a car like this before.'

'Well, we could go for a spin, but my stomach is feeling a little empty, and my favourite restaurant is only a few minutes' drive away. Are you all set?'

'Yes, Jeremy, I'm feeling a little hungry too.'

During the evening, Hannah found Jeremy to be attentive, charming and courteous. In a curious sort of way, he seemed to know all her various likes and dislikes, but Hannah knew that this could only be a coincidence. They were also so intent on getting to know one another, that they completely forgot to discuss the Iceland holiday.

Hannah discovered that Jeremy was an artist, and that he was going to be thirty the following week. 'I'm having a few friends round to celebrate. Perhaps you would do me the honour of coming as well?' he said as they were finishing off the main course. 'My flat is quite small, but it will be fun fitting everyone in.' His eyes sparkled with pleasure as he looked at her.

'Yes, I'd love to come,' Hannah said. 'Oh yes, by the way it will be my 30th birthday in a few weeks. How's that for a coincidence.'

'Wow! We're nearly the same age. Hannah, do you know, I'm really glad to have met you under London's famous clock?'

Hannah laughed. 'So am I, and I'll never again think of it as a large, but ordinary one.'

'Neither will I,' he replied suddenly reaching for her

hand. 'Now, for a little more about me. My family owns a rather nice house in outer Buckinghamshire, and I'm the elder of two sons. My parents are a little old-fashioned, and under the old rules of course, I would be the one to inherit the house when anything happens to my parents. But I'll share everything with my brother when they depart this world,' he said as a huge grin passed over his face. 'Having said that, I am extremely fond of them both. I visit them about once a week generally, and I get on with them very well.'

'It all sounds wonderful, Jeremy.'

'I have to say that my father is a little scathing about my chosen path,' he continued. 'As an artist, I don't earn a lot of money. My father feels that I'm "*Not contributing enough to society*"' he said in a pompously loud voice. Jeremy went on to speak openly about his hopes and desires for the future, and while he was speaking, Hannah had the feeling that he wanted her to be a part of his life from now onwards.

In turn, Hannah told him everything about herself, her work and her parents who lived in Hampshire. 'I'm an only child, my father is retired and my mother *"runs things"*. That's her description, not mine,' she said laughing happily. 'They live on the coast in a lovely little thatched cottage.'

'That sounds idyllic, Hannah.'

'Yes, I think it is now, because I'm bored with my job, but I used to consider it as being in the back of beyond.' Hannah paused for a moment. 'You see I'm a psychologist, and I have to delve into patients' minds and problems, which can be quite depressing at times. That's one of the reasons why I answered your advertisement.'

'A psychologist!' Jeremy pulled a face of mock horror, but it soon turned into a happy smile as he squeezed her hand. 'I'm really glad you did, Hannah. Does that mean I'll have to be careful about what I say to you?'

'Not at all. I think my profession would have driven me crazy by now if I tried to analyse everyone I meet. I've just been wondering where my life is taking me, that's all,' she said smiling at him.

At the end of the evening, Jeremy looked at her for several seconds, and Hannah couldn't help giggling playfully, which was probably the result of having drunk a little too much wine. 'Please be serious for a moment,' he said. 'I think we get on rather well together, don't we?'

'Sorry,' she said trying to suppress another giggle. 'Yes, we get on remarkably well.'

'And I know we have only just met, but I feel that we would be good together. In fact, I think we have the same views on life in general. I… I would love to get to know you even better. What do you say?'

'Yes Jeremy, I agree with you.' Hannah replied, gazing at him. She felt confused and inexplicably aware of her own desires and feelings, which had been absent for such a long time. His close proximity stirred her emotions. She'd expected to discuss a holiday in Iceland, but instead she'd found someone she could really believe in.

'So dear Hannah, I would love to go on seeing you, please.'

'I'd love to go on seeing you too, Jeremy.'

He gave her a look that made her senses reel. 'Well what about tomorrow, and the next day, and the day after…'

…And they did.

Three hectic months later they did go to Iceland, but it wasn't for a holiday. They spent their honeymoon in the best hotel in Reykjavik, and they both secretly thanked the advertisement that had brought them together. They spent their days exploring the island, walking and talking incessantly. These idyllic days passed by, and Hannah spent each night locked in Jeremy's arms, feeling serenely happy and contented for the first time in her life.

She looked forward to their future life together, knowing that she didn't need a degree in psychology to analyse her own feelings.

Hannah simply knew she loved Jeremy.

THE GREEN ROOM

Alice Barker was standing in her kitchen, when she heard the telephone ringing. She walked slowly out into the hall and lifted the receiver. Her slightly arthritic hands shook as she held it up to her ear.

'Hello,' she said, wondering who was calling her.

'Hello, is that you, Alice?'

'Yes, it is.'

'It's Andrew Martin here.' His usually cheerful voice sounded strangely mellow and sad. 'I'm afraid it's bad news for all of us, Alice. There was a meeting of the theatre's management committee last night, which I chaired. We discussed the proposed renovations to the old building, and I'm sorry to say that the bankers have turned us down. As a result, the owners of the freehold want to start the demolition process quite soon. I'm really sorry to be the bringer of such bad news.'

'Oh dear, Andrew. I can't believe it after all these years. There was talk about another theatre being built on the site if it couldn't be saved. Are they going to replace the theatre? I really hope they will. I can't believe that a town like this will have no facilities for entertainment.'

'Well no, that's not possible. It's definitely going to be made into another car park. So the final concert will be going on as planned. I thought I ought to let you know. I'm so sorry.'

Unhappy tears filled her eyes and began to trickle down her face. 'Oh Andrew, how dreadful. What a loss to the town.'

'Unfortunately, yes. The owners of the freehold have been wanting to do this for a long time. We didn't stand a chance. So, it's goodbye to the town's theatre.'

'Thank you for telling me. I'm sorry too, as I shall really

miss the old place. I won't know what to do with myself, but never mind.'

Andrew cleared his throat. 'We'll be sending you your pay cheque up to the end of next week as soon as we've sorted out what little money we have left. It won't be as much as usual, I'm afraid.'

'There really is no hurry, and I quite understand,' Alice said suddenly feeling useless and old. 'Anyway, thank you for telling me, although it's news that I would rather not have heard. Goodbye Andrew.'

The following day, Alice made her way to the doomed theatre. It was a glorious spring day and her spirits would normally have been uplifted by the thought of the warmer weather to come, but today her thoughts were too troubled.

'Morning Miss Barker, lovely day isn't it?' a young boy called out as he raced past the hall.

Alice was well known in the area and had worked in the hall for many years. 'Almost too many years,' she said tearfully as she walked up the old worn steps, and in through the large, familiar paint-flaked wooden doors. She stopped and sighed. 'I can't imagine this lovely old building being demolished. It's such a waste.' She made her way to the theatre's Green Room, which was the beating heart of the building, and she surveyed the scene before her.

'Oh dear, oh dear,' she said shaking her head sadly. 'It all looks so cold and empty.' The intense noise and the general hustle and bustle which had long been part of this room was now a thing of the past. The lingering, unmistakable smell of greasepaint, and a hint of stale perspiration remained, reminding her of earlier, happy days. Myriads of dust motes floated by in the shaft of sunlight which managed to filter in through the grimy and cracked windows.

The silence of this once busy room unnerved her. 'This room was always so alive and now look at it,' she whispered sadly. There were always lots of notices and pamphlets scattered over the walls, advertising future events, but this time she saw a new, uncreased, and pristine notice on the wall near the door. It had obviously been photocopied from the local newspaper. Alice could hardly bear to read the headline which was emblazoned across the top, just below the heading of *"THE BENDSWICH ECHO"*:

THE TOWN'S OLD THEATRE IS TO BE DEMOLISHED, AND THE SITE WILL BE DEVELOPED AS A CAR PARK!

'A car park! What do we need another car park for?' she wailed.

The floor of the Green Room was really dirty, because nobody had bothered to clean it. There was also an underlying unpleasant smell of stale perspiration, makeup, and another odour which Alice couldn't quite identify. It was littered with discarded props, broken furniture, and anything that wasn't wanted or needed anymore. The old, dark brown cracked lino had risen around the edges over the years, giving the room a neglected appearance. Alice could see pieces of broken plastic flowers, screwed up paper, hair grips, safety pins, crumbs, a broken cup, and even a hairbrush that had seen better days, peeping out from underneath an old battered table. A rotting apple core also contributed to the scene.

All this was a stark and poignant reminder of many successful shows and hurried exits. Small roundles of dust rolled around the floor, disturbed by a sudden breeze from the open doorway. What a waste of a lovely old building, she thought. No more music and excited nervous chatter and energy from performers and audiences. What memories these old walls held within their dusty, paint-flaked depths.

In her mind, Alice could still hear the voices of past assistant producers as they called out over the ancient intercom system, "Can we have all beginners on stage, please." or "Curtain up in five minutes," and "Don't forget to return all props to the Green Room, and has anyone seen the Wardrobe Mistress?"

The Dansby Memorial Theatre had been standing in the centre of Bendswich for well over a century, as it had first opened its door to the public in 1908. During those first exciting years, it had been instrumental in bringing the spectacle of the Music Hall to the town's inhabitants. Since then, they'd been treated to many different types of entertainment. There was great excitement when *"flappers"* and *"men about town"* shows had taken over. Noel Coward's plays became particularly popular, but even these were soon to be swept away by wartime entertainment, and shows put on to help the war effort.

When *"Rock and Roll"* finally hit Bendswich, it had been a signal for the young people of the town to take over. Young musicians with guitars, drums and keyboards, all sporting over-long hair, delighted the teenagers of the town by composing and playing their own brand of music. Alice had watched it all happening from the confines of the small Box Office in the corner of the foyer. 'I remember it so well,' she said sadly.

Her eyes swept around the hallowed walls of the Green Room. It was full of memories of when the theatre was really popular. Old posters and photographs of past productions overlapped one another, in order to be seen. Many were signed by the ever hopeful actors and actresses who had appeared there. Alice shook her head in despair.

The faded colours and dog-eared edges, paid testimony to their age.

She'd worked in this old place for so many years, and now her usefulness was over. She couldn't really believe it. How could she exist without it? A few tears drifted downwards, each one following the natural channels on her lined face.

Despite the owners' desperate efforts to keep the theatre open over the last few years, it's uncared for appearance, meant that the people of Bendswich eventually stayed away. The old theatre didn't stand a chance. Alice remembered the rumour that a new theatre complex might be built on the other side of the town, but nobody in the present economic climate, could afford to even start planning for such a project.

'Car parks are cheaper, I suppose,' Alice said sadly.

The final performance in the old theatre took place as planned: it was a truly memorable occasion, and once more the old walls echoed to the music of the past. Its devotees travelled far and wide to be there, and this saddened Alice even more. She viewed it all from the back row as the faded and patched red velvet curtains lurched falteringly across the stage for the last time. She couldn't help whispering, 'I can't bear it. Why, oh why, have so many people come here for this final performance, when they didn't bother to support it when the management was struggling to keep it open?'

The day after the concert was over, the staff collected everything that wasn't worth keeping, and placed it all in a skip, knowing that workmen would soon be tramping their cement encrusted boots all over the old theatre's hallowed floors. The building would then be unceremoniously stripped of all that past splendour and glory, and swiftly razed to the ground. The land would then be made ready for yet another car park.

Alice entered the Green Room for the last time. She looked lovingly at the old photograph which had always fascinated her. Its faded sepia colouring epitomised the past for her. Without stopping to think, her hands reached out, and she gently prised the photograph from the wall. She held it reverently in her thin hands, and tried to smooth the crumpled edges.

'I can't let you be destroyed after all these years,' she said, smiling down at the image of a handsome young man wearing his straw boater at a jaunty angle. His face always welcomed her into this room. 'I've no idea who you were, or what happened to you. I only know that I have to have your photograph. I can't bear to think that it will be destroyed along with everything else.'

A sudden noise made Alice jump, and she turned round.

Tom, the theatre's old cat, stood in the open doorway, looking at her. 'Oh goodness me, Tom, you scared me. What on earth is going to happen to you tomorrow, you could have been killed when the demolition people start pulling this place down? Surely the management hasn't forgotten about you?' She bent down and carefully picked him up. 'Come along my little lovely. I've got some nice milk waiting for you at my house.' Tom was used to people, but had never had a proper home, and he snuggled down into the warmth of her arms, purring contentedly.

Alice walked slowly from the Green Room with all its faded memories, and out into the dimly lit stairway which led to the foyer. She collected a few personal belongings from the Box Office, and took a final look around. Alice knew her life would never be the same again, but she was an optimist by nature.

She smiled despite everything. She now had two things

to cherish to make up for the theatre's loss: one old much loved photograph, and a warm friendly cat. Tom seemed to know that his life was about to change, and was turning to her for help. Alice looked down at him, smiled, and said gently, 'Now then Tom, you come along home with me, and we can remember all the good times together, can't we.'

For the last time, Alice turned towards the open doorway, and without looking back, she walked slowly out into the bright welcoming sunlight.

CHRISTMAS FEUD

Jennie Branham always looked forward to all the preparations for Christmas. She loved buying presents for everyone. Her excitement was instantly heightened when they started decorating the house. Jennie made endless lists of food, drink, presents and everything needed to make their Christmas perfect. Since they'd moved into the house, their final task was to tramp across a nearby field to find the most beautiful tree to be the centrepiece for their annual celebrations.

It was Christmas Eve and Jennie had just finished decorating the tree. It looked wonderful with its different coloured baubles, chocolates, and little things the children had made at school. She bent down to turn on the lights, and suddenly realised that something was missing.

Oh, she'd forgotten Fairy Belle! The children would never forgive her.

She climbed onto the chair, reached up and gave the fairy pride of place just beneath the star. Finally, she placed the presents around the base of the tree, and stood back to admire it. It was perfect.

Jennie loved everything to do with Christmas: the flickering candles, all those spicy smells, like cinnamon, and scented candles; even the smells of hot mulled wine, the turkey cooking in the oven and the wonderful aroma from the log fires. Now that nearly everything was ready, the beautifully wrapped, colourful presents, all in different shapes and sizes, seemed to vie with each other for prominence in the space under the tree. It was such a magical time.

Each year she would search for the beautiful Fairy Belle and the old Santa doll from amongst the decorations which she kept in a box in the spare room. The two dolls had been left by the old lady who'd lived and died in the house, prior to them moving in. Since then, Jennie had felt compelled to use them, but each year she'd been putting the Santa doll further to the back of the tree. She didn't like it much... in fact, it scared her.

Jennie stood back to enjoy the overall effect of the decorated tree. 'It's such a lovely tree this year. The children are going to love it,' she said happily.

Later, when her husband Mark walked into the sitting room, he stopped short when he saw the tree. 'Wow! That looks great, Jennie,' he said after walking around the tree. 'But I see that our old friend, The Scary Father Christmas is there again. I don't see why you should even keep it, let alone put it on the tree. It's frightful. Look, it's leering at us.'

'I don't like it either; it gives me the creeps, but I can't dismiss what old Mrs. Bainbridge said about them.'

'Why on earth not? It's only an old wives' tale, Jennie.'

'I know it is, but once she'd told me that if the two dolls weren't put on the Christmas tree together, some terrible disaster would happen to us, I just can't ignore it, even if you can. It may sound crazy, but...' Jennie shook her head and closed her eyes.

'Ah, togetherness, how sweet,' Mark scoffed. 'You're telling me, that you, Mrs. Jennie Sensible, believes in all that rubbish?'

'Well...'

'You do. You really do!' He laughed. 'I wouldn't have put you down as a superstitious person.'

'Well I'm not usually, but...'

'No buts, Jennie. Fairy Belle is fine, in fact she looks pretty in an old-fashioned kind of way, but... that old Santa doll is quite frightening. Look at it. It's ugly and old, and doesn't fit in with the rest of the decorations at all. The children don't like it either. Emma screamed when she saw it last year, don't you remember?'

'Yes, I do.' She sighed, 'Right you win, I'll take it off the tree, but I won't throw it away. It can go back upstairs.'

'Good, and as it is Christmas Eve, I'll go and get us a drink.'

After he'd gone, Jennie grabbed hold of the offending Santa and pulled it away from the tree. As she did so she felt a sudden pain in her hand, and dropped the old doll on the floor. Blood oozed from a tiny pin-prick in the centre of her palm, and Jennie rubbed it gingerly before picking the doll up again. She turned it over, and to her dismay, found an open safety-pin attached to the back of its grubby red coat. She pulled it out, closed it, and placed it on the table near the tree.

Later, after enjoying a glass or two of mulled wine, Jennie took the Santa doll up to the spare room and placed it back in the box. It seemed to glower at her as she closed the lid. She shook her head.

The following morning everyone woke up filled with excitement. Jennie was up first and when she walked into the sitting room, she saw something on the floor, and wondered what it was. As she walked towards the tree she noticed that it was the Fairy Belle doll, and her dress and wings were badly crumpled and dirty. Had the children been down here early to play with her? No they wouldn't do that, she thought. Then she remembered the old lady's warning, and her heart started to thump. Calm down, she told herself; there has to be a rational explanation for this, but what?

She walked out into the hall and called out to Mark, and the children upstairs.

'Could you all come into the sitting room please? There's something strange going on.'

A few moments later the excited children ran into the room followed by Mark, who was busy doing up the tie on his bathrobe.

'What's up, doc?' he quipped.

Jennie pointed to Fairy Belle. 'Just look at her, Mark,' she said in exasperation.

Mark was cross, as he turned towards six-year old, Anna. 'What have you two been doing this morning? Your mother worked so hard yesterday.'

Anna looked hurt. 'I haven't done anything Daddy. I've been asleep.'

He turned to his youngest daughter. 'What about you, Emma? Did you do this?' She stuffed two of her fingers into her mouth with dismay, and quickly ran behind the tree. 'Emma, come here please.' She peered at her father through the green branches. 'I want the truth now. Did you come downstairs this morning and do this?' Mark picked the doll up.

'No,' she said pulling a face. 'I've been sleepy too. Oh Daddy, poor Fairy Belle. P'raps it was that horrid old Santa on the treeee' she cried, as tears rolled down her face.

'Don't be silly, Emma,' Jennie exclaimed, 'I put it back upstairs last night.'

'But Mummy, he IS here,' Anna said pointing to the tree. 'Can't you see him? He's hiding amongst the branches near the top.' Jennie and Mark looked and sure enough, the old Santa doll was back on the tree!

'Right you two, upstairs and don't come down again until one of you owns up to this. Do you understand?' Mark was furious and they ran upstairs complaining loudly.

'Oh Mark it's Christmas and we mustn't be too hard on them.' She stooped down to pick the bedraggled fairy up. 'Just look at this little doll. I'll give it a wash and then I must sort out our Christmas lunch.'

146

Mark tore the Santa doll from the tree. 'This time, I'm putting you in the garden shed where they can't find you,' he said striding out of the room. Jennie felt bewildered and worried. The Santa doll had suddenly developed a character of its own, and everyone was calling the doll 'him' rather than 'it'. It was then that she noticed the pin on the floor and she picked it up. It was the same one that she'd taken out of the old Santa doll's coat the night before and... it was open again! She shivered and her heart began to thump. Questions began to form in her mind again, as she recalled the old lady's words. No, that was impossible, she thought, and hurried out to the kitchen.

Despite everything, the children were eventually allowed downstairs, happiness reigned and their celebrations began. Presents were opened with shrieks of delight, and happy hugs and kisses given. Crackers were pulled, games played, and a vast amount of food eaten, before two tired children were eventually put to bed with the problems of the morning apparently forgotten.

But not by Jennie.

They both flopped into their comfortable sofa to enjoy what was left of Christmas Day. Mark put his arm gently around Jennie's shoulders. 'Well, my love, despite a bad start, we had quite a good day, didn't we?'

'Yes we did, but...' she shuddered. 'I keep thinking about what happened this morning. It's as if the Santa doll was jealous of Fairy Belle... and... it tried to...'

'Stop right there, Jennie,' he said placing his finger against her lips. 'You've been reading too many Stephen King novels lately. The children did it and that's the only credible explanation. Put it all down to excitement, they're good kids and we are very lucky.' He kissed her warmly.

'Yes, they are.'

'And look at Fairy Belle up there on the tree. She looks

147

clean and bright again, so no harm's done,' Mark said, stretching his arms above his head.

'I suppose so,' Jenny replied quietly.

'Good. Can we forget about it now? Would you like another drink?'

'Yes please, darling. Is there any more of the mulled wine left?'

'Yes, I'll go and heat it up and then we can play a game of Scrabble perhaps?'

'Yes, that would be nice and it'll keep my mind off other things,' Jennie replied smothering a yawn.

But despite Mark's assurances about the dolls, Jennie remained unconvinced.

In the middle of the night, they were woken suddenly by the dreadful sound of the smoke alarm clanging, and children screaming. Jennie immediately made sure the children were alright, and Mark ran downstairs.

Smoke was billowing out through the sitting room door.

'Quick Jennie,' he shouted, coughing loudly. 'Get the children and go outside now. There's a fire in the sitting room. Go out the back way. There's less smoke there. Please hurry.'

'Oh my God, Mark, a fire?'

'Yes, go quickly! I'll call the fire brigade.'

Fortunately the fire was confined to the sitting room and after the firemen had left, they surveyed the damaged room. Jennie smothered a scream when she saw the Santa doll lying in front of the burnt and blackened tree. It was completely unscathed, but of the beautiful Fairy Belle, there was no trace.

'Mark,' she said her forehead creased with worry. 'You told me that you'd put the Santa doll out in the shed.'

'But I did…'

148

'So how did it get back into the house… and how did the fire…? Oh my God, old Mrs. Bainbridge's warning!'

'Don't even begin to go there, again Jennie,' Mark said in a quiet worried voice. 'We're all safe, thank God.'

Jennie was silent for a moment. 'Mark?'

'Yes,' he replied.

'When the house is back to normal, I want to move, please.'

'Move again… but why?'

'With all that happened this Christmas, I don't trust this house any more. It scares me, Mark.'

'We'll think about it darling, O.K?'

Jennie often wondered whether they'd done the right thing by leaving the Santa doll in the loft when they eventually moved out of the old house. The old doll had wreaked "his dreadful revenge" on this Fairy…

…but would that really be the end of the story?

GONE FISHING

Abigail Barton's high-heeled shoes clicked rhythmically on the old flagstone path as she hurried towards her front door. The weather had deteriorated, and it was raining hard. Her forehead wrinkled with surprise when she saw a note pinned to the area just above the letter box, and it was flapping wildly in the strengthening wind. She also noticed that her husband's car wasn't in its usual place in front of the garage.

Questions began to form in the back of Abigail's mind. Who had called here today? Where was Stephen, because he hadn't said he was going anywhere, as he rarely leaves the house at all nowadays, not even to look for a job? He'd probably gone off in a huff after their argument last night. She sighed deeply as she squinted at the note, but as her reading glasses were in the bottom of her large handbag, she decided to get inside the house before reading it.

Abigail pulled the note from the door and several large flakes of paint came off with it. She sighed again. Everything in her life was crumbling, apart from her job, which was going well. She hurried into the kitchen to retrieve her glasses.

Stephen's untidy spidery writing seemed to crawl across the paper, as she read the words… *"GONE FISHING, INSTEAD OF JUST A-WISHING…"* That was odd. Stephen hadn't used his fishing rod for ages, and as far as she knew, it was still languishing in the understairs cupboard.

A feeling of guilt invaded Abigail's mind. Their fierce argument had, much to her shame, continued before she left for the office that morning, which inevitably led them both to say even more cruel and bitter things to one another. But Stephen was out of work for the second time. She felt dreadful. He'd even intimated that she didn't love him anymore, but this couldn't be further from the truth. She loved him dearly, but he was becoming morose and disinterested in life. She knew the reason why, of course. Because he didn't have a job, he felt useless, unwanted and unloved.

Abigail often tried to tell Stephen how she felt about him, but he wouldn't listen to her, and she shook her head in dismay. She made herself a much needed cup of tea, and sat at the kitchen table sipping it miserably. When she heard the sound of some letters dropping on to the mat in the hall, she walked out to pick them up. A cursory glance proved that they were all just bills...

...apart from an official-looking white envelope addressed to Stephen.

Abigail placed them all on the table. But the white envelope intrigued her. She picked it up and turned it over. Her heart beat quickened when she noticed the company's name. Stephen had applied for a job at this company some time ago, and he'd attended an open interview, which was followed by another one a week later. Excitement flowed through her; perhaps they were offering him the job? Abigail continued to stare at the letter, desperately wanting to know what the letter contained. She agonised for several moments about whether she should open it or not.

After all, she had a right to know what the letter contained, and Stephen being out of work impinged on her life as much as it did on his, didn't it? She closed her eyes, trying to think more clearly. She had to know. Nevertheless, Abigail still felt reluctant to open one of her husband's letters. She struggled with her conscience for several minutes, before finally reaching for the envelope, slitting it open, and withdrawing the letter it contained.

Excitement rose like a tide within her, as she read it. The company was offering Stephen a really good, well-paid job! She said a silent prayer, because just recently things had become really bad and their overdraft was getting

151

larger by the day. She felt really happy for the first time in many months, and even felt like dancing around the kitchen table, until she looked at his scribbled note again.

Had Stephen really gone fishing? Abigail's forehead creased with worry. Or had he just stormed off in a rage?

Stephen had certainly been in a strange mood yesterday evening. Abigail had tried to explain that her boss, Brian Galsworthy was taking her out to dinner for purely business reasons that evening, but sadly, he wouldn't listen. Even though she loved her husband dearly, his recent jealousy had started to become a problem. He'd reacted with surprising venom, and had shouted the words... 'Well, if you feel like that then, go out with him again tomorrow night, and the next night. See if I care,' he'd said as he started to walk out of the room. 'You can even go and live with him if you like. At least he'll be able to keep you in the manner to which you've become accustomed.'

'That's not fair and you know it,' she'd shouted back at him. 'You know perfectly well why Brian invited me out this evening. We need to discuss my future involvement with the company, and there's a distinct chance that I could even be earning more money soon, too.'

'Huh,' was Stephen's petulant reply. 'I should be the main breadwinner in this family, not you.'

'Well why aren't you then?' Abigail remembered saying. *'Because I haven't got a job,'* she'd cried out in a parody of his voice. 'Grow up Stephen, you're being ridiculous.'

'Am I? Am I...?' he'd said glaring at her. 'Go on. It's what you've been wanting for a long time, isn't it, a chance to get away from me?'

'No,' she'd replied coldly. 'How can you say such a thing?'

'Quite easily, thank you,' he'd sneered with his face distorted with rage. 'Well, what are you waiting for? Go out with your precious Brian. You'll be sorry.'

Abigail's anger strengthened and bravado had taken over. 'All right, I will. Let's hope that you don't live to regret your words. I'll probably be back late so don't wait up for me.' She'd felt spiteful and wanted to get her own back on him.

She could, or perhaps should have said, 'Stephen darling, you have no reason to worry, Brian is a happily married man and his wife is expecting their first baby in about a month's time. I love you and would do nothing to jeopardise our future together.'

But she didn't.

'Have a good time,' he'd shouted sarcastically as he held his pillow covetously in his arms, before entering the spare room and slamming the door behind him.

Unfortunately, the argument had continued before she'd left for the office. Since being made redundant again, Stephen, who'd always been so supportive in anything affecting her career, was showing increasing signs of real jealousy, and this last outburst had been the final straw.

With the memory of those hurtful and angry words still ringing in her ears, Abigail had somehow managed to get through the morning, but by lunchtime she couldn't stand it any longer, and she decided to return home to try to heal the enormous rift that was opening like a chasm between them.

Abigail now sat gloomily looking at the letter on the table again. A frisson of fear passed over her. Where was he? Supposing he was doing something stupid. She raced out into the hall, opened the door of the cupboard, only to discover that his fishing tackle was still there. It was tucked neatly away in the furthest and narrowest corner. Abigail's legs began to tremble. 'So where could he have gone?'

Down to the river, perhaps, a little voice in her head suggested.

No, he wouldn't go there on his own, would he? Thoughts of impending doom began to well up inside her.

Then she remembered one of the things he'd said the night before. *"You'll be sorry,"*... and also how his eyes had flared briefly. Abigail suddenly felt cold. Surely he wouldn't do anything silly, would he? Then she began to panic: she had to find him because the letter contained a lifeline for them both. She quickly stuffed it back inside the envelope and put it in her handbag, before racing out of the house.

It only took Abigail five minutes or so to drive to the small car park that backed on to the river. The area had been a favourite of theirs for years, and as she parked her car, her heart beat quickened as she recognised Stephen's car, which was parked haphazardly in one corner of the car park.

Abigail hurried along the towpath completely ignoring the peace and the quiet of the area. It had at last stopped raining; the weather prior to that morning had been more wet and windy than usual. The birds were singing, the bees were buzzing and the dragon flies hovered over the fast flowing river. Weeping willows trailed their branches into the moving water, and a sudden flash of tawny gold caught her attention as a trout came to the surface, before disappearing again.

Normally all of these things would have heartened Abigail, but she only had one thing on her mind and that was to find Stephen. After about ten minutes, she came to the old stone bridge where they used to play Pooh-sticks together. This marked the end of the quieter section of the river, because from then on it boiled angrily over large stones until it reached the weir... and the deeper water beyond.

Abigail didn't even like to think about the weir: the river was swollen by several days of heavy rain. It was flowing rapidly, gurgling and sweeping up everything in its path. She was frantic with worry. In the distance she could

154

hear the sound of thundering water… and also the figure of a man standing on the edge of the weir. He was leaning over towards the water!

Please don't let it be Stephen.

Abigail began to run even faster. Her lungs felt as if they would burst with the effort, but she had to keep going. As she approached the weir, her fears were confirmed. Stephen's tall, gangly frame seemed shorter, and his shoulders were hunched in an attitude of despair, as he leant out over the treacherous boiling water. She could see that he had a vacant expression on his face.

'Stephen,' Abigail called out. 'Darling it's me.' There was no reaction from him. 'Stephen, everything is going to be all right,' she shouted as she rushed towards him.

He turned towards her, his eyes wild and staring. 'Go away,' he screamed, taking a stumbling step nearer to the edge of the weir, where the inky black water topped with foam, swirled and boiled dangerously below him.

'Stephen, for God's sake come away from the edge,' she pleaded.

'Go away, Abigail.'

'Stephen, I love you. I really do love you. I didn't want to go out last night, but I had to, don't you see? I did it for us.'

'You mean that you did it for yourself, and him.' He leaned even further over the weir, and Abigail's heart lurched. His foot was almost over the edge.

She screamed. 'Stephen, please… please don't. It won't solve anything. What would be the point?'

'Well, you could be with him then, couldn't you?' he said as wet shiny tears cascaded down his stricken face.

'I didn't mean any of the things that I said last night, or this morning. You must believe me. I'm sorry, but you made me so angry with your pointless jealously. I really do love you, you know.'

'You don't know what true love really is. Go away and leave me alone.'

Despite the desperate drama that seemed to be unfolding before her, Abigail remembered the letter in her pocket. How could she have forgotten it even for a second? 'Stephen... Stephen darling, this came for you this morning. Please look. It's a letter offering you a really good job. You have to read it. Please?'

Just for a fleeting moment, hope flared within his eyes, and then it disappeared as quickly as it had arrived. He turned his back on her, before saying, 'I'm not interested...'

'You can't let our lives together end like this,' she pleaded.

'There's nothing left to live for,' he replied looking down at the river. 'By going out with your boss, you've made it abundantly clear that you don't love me anymore.'

'How can you say that? I do love you, Stephen. Doesn't that count for anything? And this letter, this could be a new beginning for both of us. Please, please turn round and walk towards me.' Abigail's hand shook violently as she held the envelope out to him. 'Please.'

After a few seconds, which to her seemed like an eternity, Stephen pulled away from the edge of the weir... and reached out to take the letter from her.

Abigail held her breath as he read it.

He looked up at her. 'Abi... Abi... Abi, someone really wants me. I thought I was on the scrap heap and no use to anyone.'

'Yes, they do want you... and so do I.'

Stephen looked at her. 'Do you really mean that, Abi? Do you really love and need me?' She reached out to him, and with surprising strength managed to grab hold of him. His shoulders began to heave as he tried to brush away his tears.

'Yes of course I love you. I've lost count of the times

I've said it. You have to believe me. If your new job proves to be successful, I promise you that I will give up working, and then perhaps we could start a family. It's what we've both always wanted. Now will you believe that there's never been anyone else but you?'

Stephen took her hand and staggered back on to the tow path. A look of relief spread over his features and he pulled her into his arms. 'Abi,' he sobbed, 'I'm so sorry, so very sorry. What must you think of me? I'm a pathetic failure aren't I?' He looked away. 'I don't know what came over me. I only knew a kind of blackness. I was in a very deep hole and I couldn't see a way out, but now...'

'Yes, my darling?'

'Someone believes in me. Someone out there actually believes in my abilities.'

'Someone here always believed in your abilities too, Stephen. I never doubted you.'

Stephen looked down at his feet. 'Why couldn't I see that?' Abigail opened her mouth to speak, but he interrupted her. 'Go on say it. I was too busy feeling sorry for myself wasn't I?'

'Yes, but...'

'No buts, my darling. I'm the guilty one. I doubted you. Can you forgive me, because if you...?'

'There's nothing to forgive, Stephen.'

'Abi, I never really liked fishing you know.'

'Yes my darling, I remember. Let's go home, shall we?'

Together they walked slowly back along the tow path, their arms and lives once more entwined in renewed faith... and love.

THE BEST LAID SCHEMES

Zoe Hardcastle's deeply-set blue eyes took in every detail of the room; it looked absolutely wonderful.

'Izzy, it's nearly 10 o'clock,' she called out to her friend.

'OK. I'll be out in a minute, only I'm cleaning the sink.'

'Everything's ready, isn't it?'

'What did you say? I've got the tap running.'

Zoe frowned. 'Never mind,' she called out, giving a huge sigh. 'I hope we haven't forgotten anything,' she said, 'and what if it isn't a success?'

At that moment, Izzy walked out of the kitchen wearing a pretty floral apron, the front of which was quite wet. 'Sorry, I couldn't hear what you were saying. I was running some water into the sink, and the tap was making a really funny noise. It was coming out in fits and starts.'

'I only wanted to know if everything was ready, that's all.'

'Well yes, or as ready as it will ever be,' Izzy replied cheerfully.

'Good. Well this is it… here goes,' Zoe said laughing nervously. 'Deep breaths, fingers and everything firmly crossed. Are we all set?'

'Yes, all set. I've had my fingers and everything crossed for the past week.'

'That must have been uncomfortable for you?' Zoe said looking at her friend with a grin on her face, despite feeling apprehensive. 'You do think we're doing the right thing, don't you? I hardly had any sleep last night.'

'It's a little late for that, Zoe love, we're about to open. You must stop worrying, I'm sure everything will be fine, believe me.'

Zoe had always wanted to be a cook, or to be involved

158

in some form of catering, but her family had encouraged her to study commerce instead. She'd attended college diligently, and much to her and everyone's surprise, had eventually become a successful Recruitment Consultant in London. But deep down, she still wanted to be a successful cook. That is, until she'd met Harry, and fell deeply in love with him. Soon after their wedding day, any thoughts of a career in recruitment, or catering, quite simply disappeared.

Now, two houses and two children later, Zoe's dreams were at last coming to fruition, but instead of enjoying it she was feeling incredibly flustered. In all her forty-one years, she couldn't remember ever feeling so nervous before. She adjusted her apron and retied the ribbon around her slim waist, before pushing back an errant lock of light-brown hair from her forehead. 'There's so much at stake,' she told herself.

Three weeks ago, a thick cloud had begun to hover over their dream project. Up until then, Harry had given her loads of love and encouragement, and had invested some of his savings in the new venture. Everything seemed to be going really well, and Zoe was feeling happy. But when Harry came back from his office early, Zoe realised that something was wrong.

'Hello my love,' she'd said giving Harry her usual kiss on his cheek.

'Zoe... I... I don't know how to tell you this,' he said, as tears gathered in his eyes. 'I've been made redundant. I'm so sorry.'

Zoe remembered that dreadful day so well. She loved Harry deeply, and she knew it was imperative that their new venture should succeed. 'If it doesn't, who will pay for the mortgage or any of the other bills that keep arriving with monotonous regularity? The children are growing rapidly and they need new clothes, trainers and money for school trips,' she whispered.

Zoe looked up at the clock again. 'It is going to work isn't it Izzy?' she asked her friend, giving a nervous grin.

Izzy stared affectionately at her from behind her owlish glasses. 'For the umpteenth time, yes,' she replied. 'It's got to, after all we've both invested a lot of love, time and money in it. Peter for one, will never forgive me if it doesn't. Shall I open up?'

'Yes... yes, of course, Izzy. but it will have to be without a fanfare?'

Izzy looked at her friend and smiled, before walking over to the door and turning the notice round. It displayed the word 'OPEN' to the outside world. Zoe took a deep breath and pressed a button on her cassette player. The gentle sound of light music wafted around the room, and her heart began to pound.

The pretty little **TASTY SNACK CAFE** was at last open for business.

The café looked perfect. Each table wore a pristine, new white tablecloth with a smaller pink one placed on top. Everything matched beautifully. Cups, saucers, condiment sets and cutlery were all precisely laid out. Small bud vases containing freesias sat in the centre of each table, and their sweet delicate perfume drifted deliciously around the room. The two attractive bay windows were framed with chintz curtains held back by green satin ties with acorn shaped tassels. The windowsills were resplendent with pot plants and cards wishing them good luck with their new venture.

Zoe still couldn't quite believe that they'd actually completed everything they'd planned to do. After months of hard work, all their dreams had become a reality, and despite all her worries, she was really proud of their

160

achievements. Now, she wondered, would anyone come in?

'Harry said that we shouldn't expect too much from our first day,' she said looking pensive, 'You do think we have enough food and milk, don't you?'

'Yes of course,' Izzy assured her. Zoe looked at her. They'd been friends since their school days. Izzy was round in body and mind, but despite her encouraging words, even she was now wearing her concerned face. 'Would you like some coffee?' Izzy suddenly blurted out. 'I'm having one. My mouth feels really dry.'

'Mmmm… yes, I would, thanks.'

'And would you like a slice of cake, or a scone with lashings of cream to go with it, perhaps? They are free.'

Zoe couldn't help laughing. 'No Izzy, those are for our customers, not for us.' Izzy was looking longingly at the plates of scones and cakes which were laid out inside a see-through cold counter in front of her. 'But don't let me stop you from having one.'

'No, no I won't, but I just thought…' Izzy said balefully.

An hour and a half later, they both sat rather forlornly at one of the tables near the counter, drinking their third cup of coffee. Not one single customer had walked through the door.

'Perhaps Harry was right,' Zoe said draining the last drop from her cup, and placing it on the counter. 'Perhaps we should have advertised a little more, but it would have been so expensive.' Before Izzy could reply, the small antique bell over the doorway jangled. 'Quick, action stations, someone's actually coming in,' she whispered. Izzy stood up and walked behind the small counter. Zoe stood with her pencil and notepad eagerly poised, but inside her heart was beating away like a piston-engine.

But, it wasn't a customer, just a passer-by wanting to know where Fletcher Street was?

Their disappointment was obvious, as they both sighed in unison, and turned away. Ten minutes later the bell jangled again, and hope flared instantly between them. A young woman walked in fiercely holding onto a little boy of about five with one hand, and a bulging shopping bag in the other. The boy's face looked tear-stained and upset.

'Sit down there and be quiet,' the woman said to her son. 'I've had quite enough of your tantrums today.' She looked really tired, and her face had turned a nasty shade of puce due to the stresses and strains of being a mother.

'Don't want to,' the boy said, as he looked away.

'I don't care what you want.' She picked him up and thumped him down on a chair. 'I'm having a drink, so sit down here and shut up,' she hissed.

'Don't want to,' he repeated, mutinously kicking out at the nearest table leg.

'Can I help you?' Zoe asked, giving the table leg a hasty inspection; there was now a small dent in the white freshly painted woodwork.

The woman's forehead was creased with pain. 'I'd like a cup of decaffeinated coffee please, and make it a large one. I need it,' she said. 'I have the start of a migraine headache.' Zoe felt disappointed. Their first customer was not quite who they'd envisaged. 'I'm sorry madam,' she said softening her tone, 'but we don't have any decaffeinated coffee at the moment. Would you like a latte, or a café Americano, instead? Or we could make you a cup of tea. We've got most of the different types of tea… with lemon… and…' Zoe's voice trailed off, when she saw the young woman's look of disapproval.

'Oh just give me what you have,' she said shaking her head. 'I can't sit here arguing with you, as I've had more than I can cope with from him,' she said. She turned round to look at her child. 'Lloyd, sit still you naughty little horror, or I'll tell your father when he gets home.' Lloyd had lifted up the delicate bud vase, and had poured most of the water out on to the clean tablecloth. His small hands were just now busily detaching each little freesia bud from its stem.

Zoe was horrified. 'Please don't do that!' But Lloyd didn't stop. At the same time, Zoe noticed that one of their brand new china salt dispensers, was now teetering on the edge of the table. In sheer desperation, she turned to his mother. 'Could you ask him not to touch anything else please?' Just in the nick of time, Zoe reached over and pushed it away from the edge.

'Well if that's the way you feel you can keep your latte, or whatever it's called.' With that the woman picked up her shopping bag, grabbed hold of her protesting child, and stormed out of the cafe.

Izzy had watched the whole episode from behind the counter. She walked round and placed her arm around Zoe's sagging shoulders.

'Oh Zoe love, what a disaster, I can't believe it. I hope our future customers won't all be like that.'

'I doubt it, but just look at the dreadful mess that child made, and they were only in here for a few minutes.' Tears began to spring from the corner of Zoe's eyes. 'Do you know, that woman looked seriously over the edge, and with a child like that, I'm not surprised. We'd better clear up this mess in case someone else comes in.'

A few seconds later the doorbell jangled, and three well-dressed women entered, chatting excitedly. Izzy took up her position behind the counter, and gave Zoe the thumbs up sign.

Zoe was soon in a complete panic. 'Oh no, Izzy, look they're making their way to the spoiled table, with its bruised and broken contents strewn all over the tablecloth,' she said. 'What on earth will they think? This isn't the way

163

we'd planned things at all. It's all going dreadfully wrong.'
Harry's sad face hovered in front of Zoe. 'No, I'm not
giving up. This little shop will be a success.'

She took a deep breath before saying, 'Good morning,
ladies. Excuse me. Would you like to sit over here?' She
managed to steer them over to one of the tables in the bay
window.

'Yes, this will do splendidly,' one of them declared.
'Well girls, what shall we have? Coffees all round?'

'Yes please,' the others chorused.

'Good. Can we have three ordinary coffees please, and
some of those gorgeous scones over there? Are they home-
made?'

'Yes they are madam, and we are offering all our
customers free cream and jam scones with every coffee
today. I won't keep you long.' Zoe heaved a huge sigh of
relief, and winked at Izzy as she handed the order to her.
She was sure that from now onwards everything would be
fine. All that baking over the last few days wasn't going to
be a complete waste of time after all.

A few moments after she'd served them, one of the
women who was wearing a large blue hat that wouldn't
have been out of place at Ascot, called out, 'I say, do you
think we could have some cream with our coffee please,
only this milk is a little thin?'

'I'm dreadfully sorry, but that's all we have,' Zoe
replied reluctantly.

'Oh well, I suppose that will have to do,' she said
pulling a face as she turned round to resume her
conversation.

'I need a glass of water,' Izzy said, and quickly escaped
into the kitchen.

Zoe was beginning to wonder what else could go
wrong. She'd thought that there might be a few small

problems, but two lots of awkward customers on their first day, was quite beyond her expectations.

As if tempted by Fate, she heard Izzy cry out, 'Oh my God, Zoe! You'll never guess what's happened now. I don't believe this.'

'If it's bad news, I don't want to know,' Zoe said under her breath.

Izzy came out of the kitchen holding a glass of murky brown liquid. 'Before you say anything, it's not cold tea,' she said miserably.

'What is it then?'

'It's what's left of our water! It seems to have been turned off. Now what are we going to do?' Izzy was reduced to tears, and was holding a tissue up to her nose. 'I thought the tap was making a peculiar noise, earlier. Now I know why.'

Zoe was speechless. In the background, a voice from the C.D. player was singing '...pack up all your cares and woes...' She turned it off with a pained expression on her face. Almost at the same time, the shattering and unmistakable sound of a pneumatic drill could be heard outside in the street.

Izzy peered out of the window. 'That's why there's no water. They're digging up half the street. Oh, they can't do this to us at least not on our first day,' she wailed. 'They could have warned us, Zoe.'

Zoe's face suddenly reddened, and she closed her eyes. 'They may well have done. I'm afraid there are a few letters, and flyers under the counter there that I haven't had time to open, or even look at. They do usually warn people before turning the water off. I can't believe this has happened.' She slumped down on one of the chairs. 'Well that's it. We'll have to close. We can't possibly make tea or coffee or even wash up, without water. And listen to that noise? I can hardly hear myself think!'

165

'You're right,' Izzy replied gloomily. 'What a shambles.'

They both looked out of the window at the scene of growing devastation and chaos in the street outside. Zoe walked over to where Izzy was standing, and put her arms around her heaving shoulders. 'Izzy, my love, it won't always be like this I'm sure. We'll get over this once the water is turned back on.'

'I hope you're right, Zoe. I would hate to think that our little enterprise is going to fail. We've both worked too hard trying to make it a success.'

'Excuse me.'

Zoe had completely forgotten that they still had three customers in the café, and one of them was standing behind her chair. 'Yes,' she answered, immediately anticipating more criticism. 'Can I help you?'

The woman smiled at her. 'We understand, after reading some of your cards on the shelf over there, that this is your very first day. We're so sorry that we complained. Am I right in thinking that you haven't any water now either? We saw the men working in the road before we came in.'

'Yes, it's been turned off, and we are going to have to close the shop until the water company finishes the work,' Zoe replied.

'Is there anything we can do?' the woman said looking around her.

'I don't think so, but thank you for offering to help,' Zoe replied knowing that there was nothing they could do without water. She looked around the tea shop and tears began to collect in the corners of her eyes. Never in her wildest dreams, did she think that their first day would end up like this.

'Oh dear, what a dreadful thing to happen on your first

day,' the woman said patting her gently on the arm. 'If it makes you feel any better, we all really love this little cafe and we were thinking of holding our weekly meetings here. We think that the setting is perfect for us. There are usually about ten of us and we simply chat about various things over coffee, or a light lunch. We could also recommend it to some of our other friends as well. This town needs somewhere like this, and your scones are absolutely delicious.'

Zoe and Izzy looked at one another in delight and surprise.

'Why yes, that would be wonderful,' Zoe said. 'And we're so sorry about the milk, and not having any cream. We thought we had everything covered, and as far as the lack of water is concerned, we really have no control over it whatsoever.'

They all laughed.

After the women had left, Zoe put a notice on the door saying that they'd had to close, but would be reopening again the following day. The workmen had assured them that the water would be back to normal by then. They had just started to clear up, when there was a knock on the door. Zoe peered through a gap in the curtains. A young girl from the nearby florist's shop stood on the doorstep holding a large bouquet of flowers under each arm, and Zoe unlocked the door.

'These are for you,' the girl said handing the flowers to her.

'Thank you, they're beautiful.' Zoe closed the door thoughtfully. One was addressed to Izzy and the other one to her.

Izzy came over when she saw the flowers. 'What's this, a consolation prize and we certainly need one of those? Who are they from?'

167

Zoe opened the small card attached to her bouquet. 'Oh how sweet, it's from Harry. He says that he hopes our day is going smoothly, and sends lots and lots of love.' She noticed some more writing at the bottom of the card, which read... *'Darling Zoe, I'm sure that you'll be delighted to hear that the company who interviewed me last week have just offered me the job. Harry xxx'*

'Izzy, Harry has a job. I can't believe it, after the day we've had.' Zoe looked at her friend and smiled. '**And that is the power of love**...', she said with a twinkle in her eye.

'Mine's from Peter, wishing us both good luck. Oh Zoe, if only they knew...!' They were both silent for a few moments and then Izzy's face suddenly lit up. 'I've got an idea.'

'What sort of an idea?'

'Well, you know that old quotation about "The best laid plans o' mice and men", we could alter it just a little bit. What do you think of "The best laid plans of naughty little boys and water companies will definitely not deter us",' she said with a cheeky smile on her face. 'We could make it our motto, frame it and put it up on the wall, for everyone to see.'

'Yeee-ess,' Zoe shouted triumphantly, as they were both convulsed with uncontrolled laughter.

'Roll on tomorrow.'

**"Love conquers all things:
Let us too, give in to love."**

(Publius Vergilius Maro – Virgil 70-19 BC)

OTHER PUBLICATIONS BY BRIDGE HOUSE

Because Sometimes Something Extraordinary Happens

by Debz Hobbs-Wyatt

Seventeen short stories by Debz Hobbs-Wyatt from over a decade of competition wins and shortlistings. Featuring *Learning to Fly*, winner of the inaugural Bath Short Story Award; *Chutney*, shortlisted in the Commonwealth Short Story Prize, and *Pushcart* nominated, The Theory of Circles.

Meet a mixture of beguiling narrators, from seven-year-old Leonardo Renoir Hope trying to change the past so his dad doesn't die, and George and his carrot-growing friends on an east London allotment waiting for the world to end, to Amy Fisher who realises that her husband, after his sudden death, is not who she thinks he is… but who is the other Mrs Fisher? This one adds a touch of medical horror to the mix.

All of the stories are about ordinary people when extraordinary things happen to them.

Order from Amazon:

Paperback: ISBN 978-1-907335-69-3
eBook: ISBN 978-1-907335-70-9

A Place to Be

by Jesse Falzoi

In this haunting collection, one of Jesse Falzoi's characters imagines the word "Wuthering" means "From all directions and never the one you anticipated." Using this definition, these are Wuthering stories, coming at life from many angles, each one full of surprise and illumination. Falzoi's characters thrum with yearning –for connection, for meaning, for a place to be, to belong. They will find a permanent home inside your heart.

"This is a gifted debut. Stories which are so light and confident in their presence we can only marvel at how deep they delve into the hearts of their characters."
Mike McCormack, author of Solar Bones

Order from Amazon:

Paperback: ISBN 978-1-907335-65-5
eBook: ISBN 978-1-907335-66-2

www.ingramcontent.com/pod-product-compliance
Lightning Source LLC
Chambersburg PA
CBHW072356190626
46811CB00019B/901